'So wha...   ...d Jake, stabbing the ...   ...o funny?' Before I could reply he hollered, 'Everything's a big joke to you, isn't it? And you think you're so funny. Well, actually, you're not.' He was saying this so loudly that people were coming over towards us. 'You just love yourself, don't you?' Jake practically screamed at me.

'I didn't mean . . .' I began. But I couldn't say any more as Jake had rushed at me and sunk his ... into my stomach. I pitched forward, gasping for breath.

... e whispered in my ear, 'This is war now.'

How many Pete Johnson books have you read?

Funny Stories

THE BAD SPY'S GUIDE
*Shortlisted for the 2007 Blue Peter Book Award
Book I Couldn't Put Down category*
'This book grabs you from the first page (5 stars)'
Sunday Express

HELP! I'M A CLASSROOM GAMBLER
*Winner of the 2007 Leicester Our Best Book Award
Winner of the 2007 Sheffield Children's Book Award
(shorter novel)*
'A real romp of a read that will leave readers ravenous
for more' *Achuka*

HOW TO TRAIN YOUR PARENTS
'Makes you laugh out loud' *Sunday Times*

TRUST ME, I'M A TROUBLEMAKER
*Winner of the 2006 Calderdale Children's Book of the Year
(Upper Primary)*

RESCUING DAD
'Most buoyant, funny and optimistic' *Carousel*

Thrillers

AVENGER
*Winner of the 2006 Sheffield Children's Book Award,
Children's Books, shorter novel
Winner of the 2005 West Sussex Children's Book Award*
'Brilliant' *Sunday Express*

THE CREEPER
'Explores the subtle power of the imagination'
Books for Keeps

THE FRIGHTENERS
'Prepare to be thoroughly spooked' *Daily Mail*

THE GHOST DOG
Winner of the 1997 Young Telegraph / Fully Booked Award
'Incredibly enjoyable' *Books for Keeps*

TRAITOR
'Fast-paced and energetic' *The Bookseller*

PHANTOM FEAR
Includes:
MY FRIEND'S A WEREWOLF *and*
THE PHANTOM THIEF

PETE JOHNSON

Illustrated by
David Wyatt

CORGI YEARLING BOOKS

AVENGER

A CORGI YEARLING BOOK : 9780440864585

First publication in Great Britain

Corgi Yearling edition published 2004

5 7 9 10 8 6

Set in Perpetua by
Falcon Oast Graphic Art Ltd

Corgi Yearling Books are published by Random House Children's Books,
61–63 Uxbridge Road, London W5 5SA,
A Random House Group Company

Addresses for companies within The Random House Group Limited
can be found at: www.randomhouse.co.uk/offices.htm

THE RANDOM HOUSE GROUP Limited Reg. No. 954009
www.kidsatrandomhouse.co.uk

A CIP catalogue record for this book is available from the British Library.

Printed and bound in Great Britain by
CPI Cox & Wyman, Reading, RG1 8EX

www.petejohnsonauthor.com

A heartfelt thank you
to my agent, Jenny Luithlen,
for her constant support.

Each man is in his spectre's power
Until the arrival of that hour,
When his humanity awake
And cast his own spectre into the Lake.

WILLIAM BLAKE

CHAPTER ONE

'I am Avenger.'

They're magic words.

No, honestly . . . say them over and over and you'll put a spell on yourself and start acting braver than you ever thought possible.

According to my grandad.

Well, just lately, I've tested out those magic words. For the first time in my life I found myself facing a dangerous enemy, who . . . but I'm jumping ahead. And I really want to tell you about my grandad first.

You see, he was also my very best mate. Maybe you think that's a bit unusual. I suppose there aren't many people who have best friends who are fifty-two years older than they are.

But I'd better explain one thing about me. Seven months after I was born there was a little blip in my life – my dad scarpered off. I believe he went to Australia, though I've never had so much as a picture of a kangaroo from him since. Yet it didn't really matter (and I've hardly ever thought about him, in fact) because my mum's dad – Grandad – stepped in.

And one day, I remember, Grandad said to me, very seriously, 'I want you to know, Gareth, I'll always be there for you.' And I just said, 'Cool', or something like that. But I liked him telling me that so much.

Grandad taught me how to make a tree-house and how to play pool and golf. Later we went together to football matches and films and we were always making jokes about each other. I did this wicked impression of him. First time he saw it he laughed. And he didn't just go, 'Hee, hee.' He put back his head and gave a deep, rumbly laugh.

Actually, he was the first person to encourage me to do my impressions. He said I had an ear for people's voices, just like some people have an ear for music (which I most definitely haven't).

Then, two and a half years ago, Mum, my older sister Lisa and me moved to a little village in Norfolk and Grandad came as well. He'd been living on his own for centuries (Grandma died before I was born) so it seemed a great idea for him to live with us too.

I remember coming home after my first day at school and seeing Grandad waiting in the doorway for me. Straightaway we went out to the back garden and had a kick about before tea. Other days, after school, I'd find Grandad in the kitchen cooking the meal. And I'd chat away to him for ages about . . . well, everything really.

I'll tell you my absolutely favourite time with him, though: when I was all tucked up in bed and he'd come in and tell me a story. He'd sit on this rocking-chair which had originally belonged to him – but he'd donated to me – and I'd settle down, all snug and cosy, while he told me tales of 'ancient times' when he was an amateur wrestler.

Funnily enough, wrestling was the only interest Grandad and I didn't share. He'd tell me how it was the oldest sport in the world and that Henry VIII liked a good wrestle. Not to mention Richard the Lionheart, and . . . oh, he'd reel off all these names. But I just wasn't convinced. I loved hearing about Grandad's wrestling experiences, though.

He'd tell me how he used to watch these lads wrestling in the Town Hall on a Saturday afternoon and wish more than anything else that he could join them. He had the knowledge all right – he knew all the moves and throws and how not to fall on your head (very, very important). But he just had no belief in himself.

You see, Grandad was small and very scrawny and no one thought he had a chance. Especially the other boys at the wrestling club, who'd jeer and make fun of him. They were always taunting him with nasty jibes. Took away all his confidence.

Then one day he made himself a mask: black, with white stripes across it. And as I write this, I can see it hanging just above the rocking-chair – as Grandad gave the mask to me, too.

Anyway, Grandad put this mask on and called himself 'Avenger'. He said straightaway he could feel all this power building up inside him. He felt bolder and much braver. Overnight, he was transformed.

Grandad started wrestling in this mask under his new name, 'Avenger'. He amazed everyone with his skill and dynamic energy. He said (and this is the bit I really liked), 'Those who'd mocked me before as puny and weak now marvelled at my mighty, costumed figure and my fantastic feats.'

He made it sound as if he'd changed into a superhero like Spiderman or someone. And all the time he was talking he'd be so intent and excited, as if his days as Avenger were happening again right now.

Then last Spring (actually, I can tell you the date exactly – it was March 23rd) Mum was waiting for me when I came out of school, something she never normally did. And I knew straightaway it was about Grandad.

He'd gone out for his morning walk as usual, come home and then just collapsed . . . he passed away before the ambulance arrived.

The biggest blow of my life.

I knew Grandad was getting on and he'd been having a lot of trouble with his back and he'd been to the doctor's a few times, but I never expected to lose him so soon.

And I couldn't help feeling too – and this

probably sounds a bit cracked – that Grandad had let me down. He'd promised he'd always be there for me, but now he'd slipped off and deserted me.

All I'd got left of him now were my memories, his Avenger mask and two pictures on my wall. One was a photograph I took of him last year playing football in the garden. The other was a black-and-white one of him as Avenger.

Sometimes I'd look at Grandad in those two pictures and then tell him what I had got up to at school, just as I used to.

I missed him every single day. And I just felt so lonely without my best mate. I thought no one could ever take his place until one morning in September, when Jake appeared in my classroom for the very first time.

And immediately my whole life changed.

CHAPTER TWO

When Mrs Webber – otherwise known as 'Web-Head' – told us we had a new boy in our Year Six class, this was big news. Such things only happened about once every hundred years in our sleepy little village. (Yes, I'm exaggerating, but you get the idea.)

So Jake came in, doing that slouchy walk you only usually see on music videos and everyone just gawped at him.

Web-Head then asked if someone could look after Jake and help him settle down. Tim, who sits next to me and volunteers for everything under the sun, put his hand half-up. But then he saw how warily everyone else was scrutinizing Jake and sent it crashing down again.

'Oh, come on now, I've told Jake what a friendly class you are,' cried Web-Head. When teachers try and push you, that just makes everyone more determined not to help, doesn't it? So, no one moved a muscle until in the end – and feeling more than a bit sorry for the new boy – I stuck my hand up.

After which, Web-Head said I could show Jake round the school.

Jake was taller than average, with short, cropped hair and large eyes, so pale they seemed drained of any colour. They were rather starey, those eyes. And a bit weird. But only at first, because Jake was so confident and smiley that he just won you over. He didn't seem the least bit shy either.

Soon he was telling me all about his last school. 'Had a really bad rep there. The teachers just got on my nerves. I hate moany people, don't you?'

Before I had time to even open my mouth, let alone reply, he went on.

'One day I just flipped out, went completely off the rails.' He smacked his lips as if savouring the memory. 'That's why my parents have taken me right away from London and given me this fresh start. I'm a reformed character now. That's what I told them anyhow.'

All this was said in a strong, cockney accent which I was immediately copying in my head. Then, Jake asked, 'Hey, what's that awful pong?'

'Floor polish. Our school stinks of it the first few days of term.' Without quite knowing why, I laughed. He did too. And we both relaxed from then on.

Just as we were going back, Jake announced, 'Hey, you're all right, Garth.'

I made a face. 'Garth?' Then said, mock-indignantly, 'How dare you, sir, it's pistols at dawn now, for my name is Gareth.'

'Hey, sorry, man. I really meant to say Gareth as, in my opinion, Garth's a real loser's name, which you most certainly aren't.' He stretched out a hand to me. 'Good to meet you, Gareth.' He really emphasized my name this time.

As we shook hands I suddenly noticed how his fingernails were pretty chewed up, but I quickly forgot about it again. And it wasn't important at all – except it didn't quite go with his image, somehow.

We went back inside the classroom. Now, we have to sit in rows – Web-Head reckons we concentrate better like that. And the only place for Jake to sit was all by himself right at the front.

But if Jake minded being on his own at the front he didn't show it, giving everyone big, confident smiles. Soon the rest of the class were circling round him. But it was me he hung around with and when school finished he invited himself round my house for tea.

Mum made a massive fuss of him and even Lisa was fairly polite. You see – and I'm going to surprise you now – in all the time I'd lived here, over two years now, I'd never had a friend round for tea before.

Does this make me sound like a mad hermit? No, I wasn't like that (at least I don't think I was). I chatted with people at school all the time. And I got invited to things. Well, Tim asked me round his house for tea once.

I might have gone, if only Grandad could have come as well. But I didn't like to ask that. I mean, what could I have said? 'Is it all right if my grandad comes with me as he's my best mate and I know he gets a bit lonely if I leave him on his own?'

No, people just wouldn't understand, would

they? And so I got out of the habit of going round with anyone except Grandad.

Anyway, Jake got a big welcome from my family. After tea he asked me masses of questions about everyone in my class. And I could feel him concentrating really intently on my answers, just as if he were revising for an exam or something.

But I was pleased to give him a little guide to them all, even throwing in some of my impressions. Well, he just loved those and wanted more and more of them.

Later I told him a bit about Grandad. I showed him my two photographs and the Avenger mask. Jake was very interested. I went on to say, 'This is going to sound totally mad but sometimes I look at Grandad's pictures and then I talk to him, just as if he can still hear me.'

Jake patted me on the shoulder. 'I don't think that's mad at all.'

That night I was sure I'd found a true friend.

CHAPTER THREE

At break-time next day, Jake's mobile suddenly went off. He picked it up, listened for a moment, declared, 'Wrong one', and then pulled out another phone from his pocket and started talking on that one.

Two mobile phones. Now, how flashy is that?

Jake explained. 'I need two phones. One is for my general business, like doing deals, the other's for all my mates. (He made it seem as if there were about a thousand of those.)

Now a couple of people muttered, 'What a poser.' But the truth was that we were all very, very impressed indeed.

Here was someone exciting and exotic who'd landed at our school. Soon we were lapping up all his stories. So one day he'd be recounting how he'd been so seriously injured in a go-kart accident no one ever thought he'd walk again (but of course, he did). The next day we'd hear about a film premiere he'd attended, with all the stars of the film seated nearby. Of course, for us, being at a film premiere was just incredible. I mean, going to our grotty local cinema in the town (over four miles away) was a pretty big event. Never mind . . .

But Jake didn't just see stars there. He met them in restaurants and hotels, and even when he was roaming about Leicester Square or Covent Garden.

I have to admit I've only been to London twice in my life (both times with Grandad, incidentally). Other people in my class have never been there at all. So we were very impressed by Jake's knowledge of it. It was phenomenal. No other word for it.

But Jake's showing off (for that's what it was really, wasn't it?) might have got up people's noses after a bit, if he hadn't been so good at getting on with everyone too.

For instance, the day after he'd been round my house Jake went up to Kieran. Now Kieran's probably the most respected boy in my class. Everyone listens to him and he doesn't throw his weight around either. He's also the best footballer in the whole school. We're all convinced he'll be a professional player one day.

Jake asked Kieran what football team he supported.

'Spurs,' replied Kieran.

Well, would you believe it, Jake was a mad Spurs fan too. The two of them chatted about Spurs' fortunes this season for ages. And a bond was formed right away.

The only thing was, Jake had told me last night that he supported Arsenal. But when I questioned him he protested, 'Don't insult me. I've been a Spurs supporter all my life. Arsenal is the enemy, man.' He said this so positively I never said another word about it.

But Jake was always pumping me for little bits

of information about people. So after I'd told him that Gary – Kieran's best mate – was mad about *Buffy the Vampire Slayer*, suddenly Jake was too.

Jake also promised to get a picture signed by the entire cast of *Buffy* and he said he'd get Kieran the new Spurs kit. I suppose he was like a politician really, scattering promises wherever he went. And like a politician, he didn't deliver on a single one of them.

But at the time no one really noticed that. They were just so enthralled by Jake. No one seemed to care much either that Jake was nowhere near as good at football as we'd expected. Or any other sport, come to that.

He was bottom of the class in every lesson too. But he made a big effort with Web-Head. I suppose he didn't want to be chucked out of another school. He was always extremely polite to her and, now I think of it, crawled to her quite a bit too.

But, like I said, none of that mattered. Jake was a star. There's no other word to describe him. And soon he became one of the top boys of the class.

And, as Jake's mate, I found myself pushed into the centre too. This was kind of weird, as I'd never quite been in the swim of things before. In fact, the only time I really got attention was when I was doing my impressions. Everyone wanted to see those (by the way, I used to charge the younger pupils ten pence an impression. Can you believe that?).

The rest of the time though, I was this shy kid who walked about in a bit of a dream. Not on bad terms with anyone. But on the outside of things, definitely.

So was Tim, the boy I sat next to. Only Tim was also a try-hard, and really anxious to please. His nickname was Half-Boy (which he loathed) because he was the smallest boy in the class. And Tim told me once that every time someone called him Half-Boy he wanted to run away and never come back.

Most boys — and a few girls — were very patronizing towards him. But Jake never was. In fact, he was dead friendly to Tim from the start. I liked him for that and so many other things too.

Just one thing bothered me about Jake really, and that was his home — and the fact that he never seemed to want me to go inside it. He lived about a ten-minute walk away from me, in a bungalow with an immaculately kept front garden.

But the first time I popped up on his doorstep Jake didn't look exactly thrilled to see me. 'Sorry,' he hissed, 'but Mum and Dad are still tidying up and they'd go mad if I asked you in. All right if we go round your house instead?'

'Yeah, absolutely.'

Well, I didn't think too much about that. But a few days later I turned up at his house once more. Again, Jake opened the door. And again, he didn't appear overjoyed by my surprise visit.

'Can't ask you in,' he said, 'as my parents aren't very social.' At that very moment a door opened and Jake's mum appeared, beaming away at me.

'Ah, hello, are you Gareth? We've heard such a lot about you.' She couldn't have been friendlier. And neither could Jake's dad who came to say hello to me.

But there was one thing. Jake's dad walked with a stick, and looked a bit frail. Jake told me afterwards that his dad had retired early because of bad health. I wondered, was Jake a bit ashamed of his dad? Did he figure a sickly dad didn't go with his image? But that seemed very shallow. I was puzzled, though, as to why Jake was so anxious to keep me away from his parents.

On the night I'm telling you about, Jake's mum

asked if I'd like a drink. Only I didn't get a chance to reply, Jake was already pushing me towards the front door, saying, 'No, we're going off to my shed.'

And we ended up in this small shed at the end of his back garden.

'My parents let me take it over,' said Jake, so it's all mine. I call it my bunker of dreams.'

'Do you indeed?' I smiled.

Jake couldn't just call it his shed. No, he had to give it a fancy name. But I rather liked that about him.

Jake opened the bolts to his bunker of dreams. 'Should also be locked on the inside, really, I suppose,' he said. 'Anyway, come in.'

He switched on a light which cast a dim glow over everything. And what really surprised me was how little there was in this bunker of dreams: a CD-player, a few CDs, a comic, a couple of books, an apple core . . . hardly anything really. Except for one very large photograph . . . of Jake.

It was a recent one of him. And quite a good one. Jake looked dead hard and tough in it. It was right under the light too, so you couldn't miss it. And I thought, if I had a shed like this the last thing I'd want in it would be a massive picture of my ugly mug.

It did seem big-headed of Jake. Very big-headed, actually.

Jake was saying, 'This is my private place. I can come in here, switch on some music and just think. I can spend hours doing that and . . .' He stopped. He noticed how my gaze kept returning to that picture of himself.

'I suppose you're wondering why I've stuck my face up there.'

'You wanted something to scare away any wild beasts who might be nearby.'

He grinned, then said, in a small voice, 'In that photo I'm exactly how I want to look.'

'It's a good picture,' I conceded.

Jake looked away. 'No need to tell anyone else about it, is there?'

I grinned. 'All right.'

And then Jake seemed so guilty I burst out laughing. So did he.

And we didn't say much else about it. But I remember that moment very clearly.

You see, it was the very last time Jake and I laughed together.

CHAPTER FOUR

Next day I did something very, very stupid.

But what I want you to understand is— No, I think I'd better tell you exactly what happened first.

The morning in question I arrived at school early. No particular reason. I just did. Jake wasn't there as he had a dentist's appointment and wouldn't be back until break-time, so I joined the crowd in the playground who were thronging around Nicola.

She'd been away ill with gastric flu and this was her first day back this term. People were telling her all the news, especially about Jake, of course.

I was just standing near the back, not saying anything really, when Kieran said, 'Gareth is Jake's best mate, you know.'

Nicola looked pretty surprised, then said, 'Well, tell me all about him then, Gareth.'

All at once everyone was eyeballing me. I really didn't like that. As I think I mentioned, I'm actually quite shy. So I just mumbled, 'Well, he's just a top person: lively and funny—'

'And I'm told he's got a weird voice,' interrupted Nicola.

'Not weird,' I corrected. 'Just cockney.' And all at once I started doing a very brief impersonation of Jake. I'd practised it at home a few times but this was the first time I'd ever performed it in public. And everyone just went wild, demanding an encore.

Losing all my nerves now I launched into a full-scale Jake impression. One little thing I'd noticed: Jake's cockney accent wavered a little sometimes. I suspected him of exaggerating it, just a bit. So I did this too, saying, 'Most of the time I'm as cockney as the Artful Dodger, but now and again, I forget.'

Half the school were watching and cheering now. And I didn't want to stop. So I started copying Jake's highly distinctive walk and saying things like, 'I'm so cool I see films before they've even come out.'

Then suddenly people stopped laughing. Their smiles became distinctly uneasy; they shuffled about awkwardly. A cold shiver ran all the way down my spine. When I turned round, I saw Jake standing right behind me like a shadow.

'Hey, Jake,' my voice came out all high-pitched. 'We were having a . . . a bit of a laugh.' My words fell around him, but he didn't reply. He just stood there, his face struck with horror. Even writing about it now makes me shudder. It was a truly awful moment that seemed to stretch on and on.

Finally Gary called across to Jake asking why he wasn't at the dentist. Jake turned to him with this glazed look on his face, as if he still couldn't believe what he'd just witnessed. 'He was ill,' he said in a flat, dead voice. Then, without another look at me or anyone else, he stumbled away in a very un-Jake-like manner.

There was a lot of excited muttering and I heard someone say, 'Gareth definitely went too far.'

In the classroom Jake seemed to have recovered and was his normal dynamic self again. But when I grinned at him, he just blanked me. I sat on my own (Tim was away) knowing I'd made a terrible mistake. And I was so angry with myself.

It must have looked as if the moment Jake was away I was off making fun of him. But it wasn't really like that. I was just . . . well, showing off – that's what I was doing. And when you get people laughing it's so intoxicating, you'd do anything for it to carry on.

What I wanted Jake to know – and I'd really like you to understand this as well – is that I didn't mean any harm by what I'd done. That definitely wasn't my intention. After all, he was my mate. Why would I want to hurt him?

But Jake ignored me all day. Finally, at the end of the lessons, I went right up to him and said, 'I'm truly sorry for what I did this morning. I got carried away and . . . I'm sorry.'

Jake glared at me and I thought he was going to blank me again. But instead, after everyone else had left, he hissed, 'You held me up to ridicule today.'

'No . . .'

'You tore me to shreds in front of everyone.'

'Oh no . . .'

'And you betrayed me.'

'Now, hold on . . .'

But Jake interrupted, 'You're not my mate any more,' spitting those words at me before stalking off.

All evening I ran over and over my impression of Jake. I'd poked a little bit of fun, that's all. I'd gone a bit far, yes. But that stuff Jake was saying about holding him up to ridicule and betraying him . . . that was way over the top.

And anyway, friends do tease one another. Take Grandad and me. We were always insulting each other. One time I remember, Grandad said he'd gone on to the Friends Reunited website and I quipped, 'Did Moses get back in touch then?' Grandad cracked up laughing.

He, in turn, was always making rude comments about my football playing. He said I was the worst player he'd ever seen. And I'd pretend to be annoyed. But I knew he was only fooling about really.

Jake must take his image very seriously. That put me off him a bit, to be honest. But I still didn't want our friendship to break up over a silly impression.

Next day, though, Jake carried on ignoring me.

Tim was back, so I told him what had gone on yesterday.

'You were such good mates,' wailed Tim.

'I know.'

'Maybe if I tried talking to him for you . . .'

I didn't see how that could do any harm.

Tim was gone for ages. When he came back he was even more out of breath than usual.

'He's really mad at you,' cried Tim, as if he was telling me something new. 'And he's upset too.'

'I know.'

He shook his head. 'Doing it behind his back too.'

'Yeah, OK,' I said, shortly.

'Everyone thinks you went too far.'

'They were all laughing at the time, though,' I said. 'And I didn't mean any . . .'

'I know you didn't,' interrupted Tim, patting me on the shoulder. 'And Jake says he'll see you on the back field at the start of lunch.'

'Really!'

Tim's face was one big smile now, chuffed that he'd managed to broker a peace settlement.

'Hey, well done,' I said.

'He took a bit of persuading, but I think you'll be all right now. Just lay off the impressions for a bit.'

'Oh, I will.'

At the end of the morning lessons Jake sped out of the classroom and off to the back field. He must have realized I was just behind him but he didn't look back once.

He strode right to the end of the back field. Then he stood waiting for me, his arms folded across his chest. I half-ran over to him.

'Thanks for talking to me,' I began. 'I know I've upset you.'

'It's much more than that,' interrupted Jake. 'If you'd just been someone I knew a bit mocking me, it wouldn't have been so bad. But you were my mate.' His voice shook. 'So I can't ever forgive what you did.'

Now I was feeling a bit lost. What was going on? Why was Jake taking a silly impression so seriously?

'Where I come from,' said Jake, 'if a friend insults you, it's as if they've spilt your blood and you have to spill that so-called friend's blood in return.'

Jake made it sound as if he'd been in the Mafia before he'd come here. I couldn't help laughing at this. 'Oh, come on . . .' I grinned.

Jake scowled furiously. 'I thought you'd come here to apologize.'

'I have.'

'So what are you laughing about?' asked Jake, stabbing the air with his fist. 'What's so funny?' Before I could reply he hollered, 'Everything's a joke to you, isn't it? And you think you're so funny. Well, actually, you're not.' He was saying this so loudly that people were coming over towards us. 'You just love yourself, don't you?' Jake practically screamed at me.

Stung now, I shouted back, 'Well, at least I don't go sticking up massive pictures of myself everywhere.'

As soon as the words were out I wished I could have taken them back. The last thing I wanted was to get into a slanging match with Jake. And I remembered, too, how I'd promised not to tell anyone about the photograph.

'I didn't mean . . .' I began. But I couldn't say any more as Jake had rushed at me and sunk his fist into my stomach. I pitched forward, gasping for breath.

Jake whispered in my ear, 'This is war now.'

CHAPTER FIVE

'This is war now.'

The words raced round and round in my head.
It was a crazy thing to say. And what did it
actually mean anyway?

NOTHING.

Jake was just sounding off. That's what Tim and
I decided. I even hoped Jake would realize he was
totally over-reacting and would sidle shyly up to
me and say, 'Sorry for going a bit loopy. Can we
just forget it?'

That's exactly what I wanted, just to forget the
whole sorry mess. But he didn't do that. Instead,
every time I saw him, he'd fix me with his stone

gaze for a moment and then stalk off. But with everyone else he'd be as smiley and friendly and confident as ever. Only I got the big freeze.

For a couple of days nothing else happened. Then came Thursday afternoon: us boys had been playing football with Mr Matthews, the Headteacher, supervising. He'd kept us late, as usual, so at the end there was a mad scramble to get changed and go home.

Jake wasn't there. He'd hurt his leg and had a note excusing him from football (I don't actually think he enjoyed football half as much as he pretended) so he had already gone home.

Anyway Tim and I rushed out of school together. Tim's mum was waiting in her car for him, but just before he went over to her Tim sniffed and announced, 'It stinks around here.'

I could smell something bad too and agreed, 'Yeah, it's disgusting, isn't it?'

Tim dived off then. But as I walked off I noticed how that horrible smell appeared to be following me home.

I took a quick look inside my bag. Nothing remotely smelly there. Then I just happened to glance underneath it. It was caked in . . . well, at first I thought it was mud. But one whiff swiftly confirmed what it really was.

Immediately I scraped my bag up and down on the grass. It was still pretty stinky though. As soon as I got home I emptied my bag and hosed it down in the back garden.

A bad smell still lingered, so I grabbed some air freshener and squirted it all over my bag. I got a bit carried away actually. Practically used the whole can, didn't I.

And, as soon as Mum got back from work, her nostrils went into over-drive.

'Thought my bag was smelling a bit stale and needed freshening up,' I explained, hopefully.

'I see,' said Mum, smiling. 'And this urge to shower your bag in air freshener just came over you, did it?'

I could tell she wasn't buying that one (my mum's no fool), so I told her how I'd absent-mindedly slung my bag down on a load of dog dirt while I was nattering to Tim . . . She believed that tale as it's just the kind of thing I might do.

'You walk around in a dream, don't you?' she said, before adding, softly, 'just like me.'

Mum then forgot all about my bag while I could think of nothing else all evening.

I knew at once it was Jake, of course. He was the only one with a motive. And he had the opportunity. I could see it all in my head. While we'd been playing football he'd slipped back into the changing room, sneaked off with my bag, found some dog dirt (always some on the road just off our school, despite all the notices about fines), thumped my bag down in the middle of it and then returned it to the changing room.

What a sneaky, nasty, totally pathetic thing to do. OK, Jake had made my bag stink. But he'd also degraded himself, hadn't he? Do you know, I even started to feel sorry for him.

He must be really unhinged to be doing stuff like that. Then I thought about Jake some more and decided he wasn't unhinged after all. I figured it was because we'd been such good mates he was acting like this. I reckon people you like can hurt you more than anyone else. Their insults go deeper. When they do hurt you, you sort of hate them for causing you so much pain, don't you?

If only I hadn't done that impression of Jake. How often had I said that to myself. It was a deed I just couldn't undo.

But at least I needn't make it any worse. So I decided I wouldn't go off shouting at Jake tomorrow for what he'd done. He'd only shout back. And things would get even worse (if that's possible) between us.

No, I formulated a different plan. I'd be very calm and controlled with Jake. I'd say, 'I got your message in Games.' I thought that was quite a cool way to refer to what had happened.

Then I'd go on to say that we were even now, so could we start again.

Next morning I was so early I was the very first person to arrive at school. I wanted to talk to Jake before lessons started. Hours seemed to go by before I spotted him. For once he was on his own.

I went straight over. I was nervous but I really wanted to say this. 'I got your message in Games yesterday.'

That took him by surprise all right. I rushed on. 'But that message you left underneath my bag, well, it's all right because we're even now, aren't we?'

Just for a moment that hard look fell from his face. Something flickered in his eyes. Then it died again and he hissed, 'You bad-mouthed me. I'm sorry, but I just can't forgive that.'

'Why not? I've apologized,' I cried. 'What more do you want?'

His voice was hardly even a whisper now. 'I want you off my manor for ever.'

I gaped at him, then repeated, 'Your manor? Do you really think this school belongs to you now?'

He was already walking away.

'You can't decide who stays at this school,' I called after him. Then I stood there, just seething with anger and frustration. I'd tried to make peace with him today. But instead . . . well, he was acting even loonier than he had before. That was it now, though. I wouldn't be making any more effort with him.

And then, just for myself, I did an impression of Jake saying, 'I want you off my manor for ever.' I remembered, too, how his cheeks had swelled when he said it, as if intoxicated by all his power.

Just who did he think he was anyhow?

He'd only been at this school for five minutes.

I'd been here for two and a half years. And I had absolutely no intention of leaving.

CHAPTER SIX

Tim went on trying to make peace between Jake and me.

'Just come and talk to Gareth,' he said to Jake.

'Who?' replied Jake, as if the name was new to him. 'Nah, I don't have anything to do with him.' It was totally hopeless, but Tim went on hanging round with Jake.

Then one morning Jake called out, 'Hey, Tim, how's my main man then?'

Tim got so high hearing that, he couldn't sit still for the rest of the day. Web-Head kept saying, 'I don't know what's the matter with you today, Tim.'

I didn't say anything to Tim, but I guessed why Jake was throwing all those compliments his way. He was trying to take my mate away from me, wasn't he?

Now Tim rarely had any money on him. He'd either left it at home or spent it all. And at break-time, when we were buying sweets and chocolates in the dining hall, Tim would often stand beside me whispering, 'Gareth, be a mate, buy us a choccy bar. Promise I'll pay you back tomorrow.'

Sometimes I'd have to reply, 'Sorry, I just can't pay for you again today.'

But lately I'd been buying Tim chocolate and sweets every single day. And it was wiping me out. I felt as if I were suddenly in a competition with Jake for Tim's friendship. You could say I was having to pay Tim to be my mate. That's certainly what it felt like sometimes.

One day I said to Tim, 'You and Jake are becoming quite matey these days.'

'Yeah, we're getting along so well,' said Tim, proudly. Then he added, 'But don't worry, I make sure we never talk about you.'

'Oh, I couldn't care less if you do,' I replied, lying my head off.

'It's a real shame you and he haven't made up,' went on Tim.

'Not bothered now,' I said.

'And you're just about the only person who doesn't like Jake,' went on Tim.

At that moment Jake appeared, surrounded by the usual gaggle of fans. Jake called Tim's name.

'Got to go,' cried Tim at once.

'Can't keep Jake waiting, can you,' I murmured.

Tim coloured. Then he glared at me, red and irritated. 'You have to make snide comments, don't you?'

'What!' I cried. 'I just said . . .'

'I know what you said,' he snapped.

Next day I'd hung my coat up and was just going into the classroom when Tim came tearing after me and immediately spluttered, 'Can't see the chalkboard properly. Messing up all my schoolwork . . .'

'Oh, got to have glasses, have you?' I

interrupted. 'Well, don't worry, you can get dead cool ones now.'

'No, I'm not getting any glasses,' Tim cried, reddening as he spoke. 'My eyesight's not quite that bad. It's just . . .' His voice trailed off. 'I need to move right to the front.'

In an instant I got it. He was moving to sit next to Jake. Tim smiled apologetically. 'I'm going to miss sitting next to you but . . .'

'You can't see the chalkboard,' I said, dully.

Tim looked away. 'We'll still be mates though.'

'Yeah, of course we will,' I said.

I watched Tim take all the stuff out of his desk and over to the one next to Jake at the front. Everyone else was watching too – and asking questions.

'Why are you moving over there, Tim? Have you and Gareth fallen out?'

'No, of course we haven't fallen out, it's just . . .' Then he said that spiel about not seeing the chalkboard.

Later he said it all again when Web-Head asked why he'd moved, and even she didn't look as if she believed him.

Tim made a point of talking to me at break-time – even buying me a bar of chocolate too. But all the time I sensed Jake hovering nearby.

At the end of school Tim and I usually go out of school together. Today I noticed Jake walking right behind us.

'Is he your bodyguard now or something?' I asked.

'No, it's just he's coming round my house for his tea.'

I started with surprise. 'You invited him, did you?'

'I've invited you loads of times,' Tim shot back, 'and you've never bothered.'

'Hey, that's not true,' I protested. 'It's just . . . it wasn't very convenient.' My voice fell away.

'Well,' said Tim, 'when I asked Jake he said yes straightaway . . . See you then.'

'Yeah, have fun,' I murmured.

I watched Tim and Jake go over to the car. I saw Tim's mum get out and shake hands with Jake, Tim grinning ever so proudly beside him.

And suddenly Jake turned round and gave me such a smug, gloating smile.

CHAPTER SEVEN

The day Tim moved to the front, something else started.

I was answering a question in class when I heard a loud yawning noise. Web-Head heard it too and immediately demanded, 'Who is making such rude sounds?'

Jake raised his hand and smiled sheepishly at her. 'Sorry, miss, but I suddenly felt very sleepy.'

Web-Head just tut-tutted a bit but there were sniggers from several of the boys. And when I started speaking again, there were more yawning sounds from Jake — only quieter, so Web-Head couldn't quite catch them. But I did.

After that, everything I said was accompanied by yawning sounds and heavy sighing, too. I decided the best thing to do would be to just ignore it. Jake would soon get bored if I didn't react.

But unfortunately something quite different happened. Just as every boy in the class copied Jake's slouchy walk, so they also copied his sound effects too. And soon my talking would be the signal for yawning to break out all over the classroom.

Occasionally Web-Head would overhear this and say, sharply, 'I'm very sorry someone finds my lessons so boring.' She never worked out that I was the inspiration for those noises.

Then Jake added a new sound to his repertoire. He didn't just yawn whenever I spoke. He'd whisper a name too: *Garth*. That was what he'd called me by mistake that very first day. And then he'd apologized by saying, 'Garth, in my opinion, is a real loser's name.'

Before long half the class were whispering, 'Garth, Garth,' alongside anything I said.

Can't tell you how much I hated that. That bugged me far more than the yawning noises, but I went on pretending I couldn't hear any of it.

Then Jake did something so funny I forgot to laugh. He put itching powder all over my clothes in Games. So when I dressed again I was scratching and itching frantically. All the boys who'd been in on the joke were beside themselves. They couldn't stop laughing. I attempted to look amused too, but I knew this wasn't just a harmless prank. Jake was trying to turn me into an object of scorn and derision. He was starting to succeed too. Inside, I was seething.

Still, I bottled up all my frustration until one day in Games, when we were choosing football teams. I was the last person to be chosen (even though I'm quite a decent player – and better than Jake any day, if I say so myself) which was pretty insulting. But then I heard Gary say, 'And we've got Garth.'

All at once I shrieked, 'It's *Gareth*, not Garth.' My voice had gone all high-pitched, and I sounded like a petulant little girl. Of course, immediately everyone started mimicking me, saying, 'I'm Gareth, not Garth,' in squeaky, tremulous voices.

I knew I'd made an absolutely critical mistake. I'd shown a weakness. They knew where my vulnerable spot was now.

Soon it wasn't just when I spoke that I'd hear, 'I'm Gareth, not Garth.' It was chanted all day long. Pupils in younger years would also call it out as I went past, then fall about laughing. Even girls began to join in.

I was just so bewildered. You see, although I was fairly quiet, I'd never been picked on or made fun of before. I had quite a good reputation, actually. But that was all just dissolving away. I went on acting as if it wasn't happening. If I didn't respond maybe it would all just go away. Perhaps that sounds a bit pathetic but I just didn't know what else to do. And, of course, things got even worse.

People even started looking at me differently. I'd catch them glaring at me suspiciously . . . what on earth was going on?

I asked Tim, but he just shrugged and muttered that he didn't know what I was talking about. There was never time to say anything else. I only ever had very brief chats with Tim these days.

Then one day, I saw my chance to swing back into favour again. It happened in registration. Web-Head was trying to explain something when some of the girls started talking.

Now Web-Head absolutely hates that. 'I know this – you don't,' she bellowed. She went on to say how she'd never taught such a badly behaved, poorly motivated class. The atmosphere, as you might imagine, was distinctly grim after that.

Then she had to go outside for a moment, leaving us to read in silence. To lighten the atmosphere I charged up to the front and said, 'How dare you start talking when I'm speaking to you. This is not acceptable behaviour.' Now my impression of Web-Head in a foul mood is one of my best. I even copy the way she blows through her nose like a horse when she's telling someone off.

So I stood, waiting for the laughter . . . that never came. Tim grinned a little. But otherwise, nothing, except a vast, deafening silence.

Panicking now, I launched into what you might call my party piece – my impression of Quasimodo. Apart from teachers, I get more requests for this one than any other. And I hadn't done it for a while.

I twisted my face right up and lumbered about muttering: 'The bells, the bells.' Not a ripple.

Then Jake let out a loud yawn. And like a series of echoes, the yawn was repeated all over the room.

Well I just slunk back into my seat, burning with shame. It wasn't only that no one laughed — it was the way the whole class seemed to despise me. In that moment I felt as if all my confidence and all my sense of fun had been knocked right out of me.

Then Web-Head reappeared. It was maths now. I got out my book in a daze, not really looking at it. But the girl on the next table did, snatching my exercise book away and calling out, 'Who likes Barbie then?'

I was totally bewildered — until I saw that my maths book was covered in Barbie stickers. What on earth . . . ? Then I saw Jake's nasty smile. He'd sneaked into the classroom and done that. It wasn't just my maths book he'd covered either. Barbie stickers decorated every one of my exercise books.

The whole class was sniggering now. 'What is the matter with you all this morning?' asked Web-Head. Then she noticed my maths book. She held it up in the air. 'I'm sorry, Gareth, but I do not find this funny. I'm very disappointed in you. You'll stay in at break-time and re-cover every one of your exercise books.'

What she didn't notice was that on every exercise book *Gareth* had been changed to *Garth*.

GARTH!

The person who Jake was trying to change me into: *Garth* – the outcast. *Garth*, the class pariah. *Garth*, the big joke.

That wasn't me. So why was everyone acting as if it was? I had to talk to Tim, find out why everyone was acting so strangely to me.

But Tim was with Jake all day. My only chance came at the end of school. Jake had already left with a large gang, as usual. Tim was busily packing up.

'Tim?'

'In a bit of a rush now,' he said, making for the door. 'You know my mum goes mad if I keep her waiting. See you tomorrow.'

'Just tell me one thing then,' I asked.

Tim had his hand on the door.

'Why is everyone turning against me?'

'They're not,' said Tim, but he'd turned round and was walking back over to me.

'Come on, Tim, you know they have. They keep giving me all these really, dirty looks . . .'

'It'll blow over,' interrupted Tim.

'What will?'

Tim shifted about awkwardly, then hissed, 'You have been saying stuff about people and I know you were just trying to be funny . . .'

'What stuff?' I demanded.

'You know.'

'No, I don't.'

'Oh, come on, you did an impression of the whole class for Jake, didn't you?'

'Yes,' I agreed, cautiously.

'Then you said some things too. And Jake . . . well he thought people had a right to know what you'd been saying behind their backs.'

'So what am I supposed to have said?' My voice rose, it was almost a shout.

'I don't know exactly . . . well, you said something about me.'

'What?' My whole body was stiff and tense now. 'Come on, tell me.'

'That you need water wings every time I speak because I spit so much . . . I suppose it is kind of funny but it's . . .'

'I've never in my life said that,' I interrupted.

'Are you sure?' he asked, not believing me.

'I swear on my life I didn't.' I said this so definitely Tim gaped at me.

The classroom door opened. Jake was back. 'You all right, Tim?' he asked.

'Oh yes, yes,' he cried.

'Only there's something I need to run past you,'

said Jake. 'Something important.' He left again without closing the door.

'Do you believe me, Tim?'

'Look, it's not important.'

'Yes it is. Do you believe me?' I persisted.

He hesitated, then nodded. 'Yes,' he mumbled, before sprinting towards the door. 'But I've got to go now.'

'Jake's making up lies about me,' I cried after him. 'And you're all believing them.'

But Tim never answered. He didn't even look back.

CHAPTER EIGHT

The first thing I did when I got home was to tell Grandad what had happened.

I imagined him listening to me, sitting in his chair in my bedroom just as he used to. And then, very softly, I asked, 'Grandad, where exactly are you now?'

I remember, at his funeral, this poem was read out. I think it was supposed to be comforting, but I didn't care for it at all. It spoke about Grandad 'going faraway into the silent land.' Part of my mind went with him. And right away I realized Grandad would hate it there as he just loved talking. I knew how lonely he would be too.

So that night, I whispered, 'Grandad, if you can hear me, don't waste your time in that silent place. Come back here, with me.'

And later I did see him, but only in a dream.

I was dashing on to a railway platform. A train was leaving. An old one, actually, with lots of steam — just like the ones Grandad used to tell me about. And then, through the steam I saw a face staring out of the window. 'Grandad!' I yelled his name. His face lit up. He waved madly, but the train was already leaving.

'Grandad, I've got to talk to you,' I screamed, tearing after the train. I couldn't catch it in time. I stared dejectedly after it, and then I woke up.

I gazed around me. It was the middle of the night. The darkness was really deep and thick. It had turned icy cold as well.

And then, through the darkness, I noticed the rocking-chair. It was moving, just as it used to after someone had got up from it. But no one could have been sitting in it, could they?

'Grandad?'

I shot up in bed. I looked all around me. No one was here now, but I had the strongest feeling someone had been.

Had Grandad somehow picked up my distress signal and crept back to check up on me?

'Grandad,' I whispered, 'if you can hear me, come back – and stay and talk to me next time. I promise I won't be at all scared.'

CHAPTER NINE

The teasing and taunting went on and on. Web-Head didn't notice any of it. It was all smuggled past her. But every day more invisible blows rained down on me. There was never any let-up.

I didn't get a chance to chat with Tim either. Jake was always there. In fact, he was everywhere. Each day his smile seemed to grow wider, his voice louder.

I tried asking Kieran and a few of the girls if Jake had accused me of saying things about them. But their eyes just slid away from me. I heard one girl mutter, 'He can't start denying it all now.'

I couldn't even find out what I was supposed to

have said. It was like fighting in a fog. It was hopeless.

Do you know, some mornings I'd stand outside the school gates, my knees trembling away, just as if it were my very first day there. Then I'd tell myself not to be such a baby and I'd totter inside.

But all the bad vibes were really starting to get to me. And some days I just felt so totally worthless that I couldn't be bothered with anything.

One afternoon Web-Head asked for volunteers for a talent show at the school. Normally I would have been in there like a shot. But once humiliated, twice shy, so I just stared down at my desk.

Web-Head said, 'I thought you'd be treating us to some of your impressions, Gareth.' (Yes, even the teachers knew about them.) But behind me came whispers of, 'Garth, Garth, Garth.' I just shook my head dismally.

I felt that not doing my impressions meant I'd lost the point of myself. There was nothing to stop me shrivelling into Garth now.

I sat in class so quietly I might not have been there at all. And people acted as if they couldn't see me either, often looking right through me. I had become the invisible boy.

Until one day when I decided I'd had enough.

It was a really small incident which finally roused me, too.

On the day I'm telling you about, another new person joined our class (two in one term – that must be a record).

It was a girl this time, Alice: she had long brown hair and was quite pretty really. She smiled nervously at everyone – even me – and patiently answered all the questions that were fired at her. She'd lived in Biggleswade before she'd moved here with her mum, step-dad and half-brother, Jules, aged only two. Her top hobby was football . . . both watching and playing it . . . All morning she was questioned and Jake hardly left her side. At the start of afternoon school he announced that he'd be asking Alice out soon. Already he seemed to be working his charms on her. Trust Jake to get a nice girlfriend like her.

Anyway, a bit later that afternoon a note was passed round. I saw Alice reading it – then Kieran . . . but it missed me.

Of course that meant one thing, didn't it: the note was about me. I bet it had come from Jake too. What lie was he circulating about me now? Everyone – including Alice – would, of course, believe it. Anger welled up in me.

I looked around. The note had reached Nicola.

Suddenly I jumped up, grabbed my pencil and made as if I was going to sharpen it over the bin. But on the way I snatched the note right out of Nicola's grasp. She let out a startled yelp.

Web-Head's eyes snapped up from her marking. I quickly covered the note in my fist. 'Sit down now please, Gareth,' she murmured. Then she resumed her marking.

I went back to my seat. I could feel thirty pairs of eyes watching me as I opened the note and read: HAVING A PARTY FOR ALICE AT MY HOUSE ON SATURDAY. EVERYONE INVITED — EXCEPT GARTH. SO KEEP THE PARTY A SECRET FROM HIM. JAKE.

Tears of indignation started in my eyes. Well, I would turn up at that party all right, with a whole load of eggs which I'd throw at everyone as they went inside. No I wouldn't. I'd send Jake a parcel, but not say it was from me. He'd open it up, discover a stink bomb inside . . .

No I wouldn't. I'd . . .

I was still plotting my revenge on Jake when the bell went. Web-Head had to go to a meeting, but for once the rest of the class didn't rush away. They were watching me pick up the note and walk over to Jake's desk with it.

I tore the note into tiny pieces and scattered them all over Jake's desk. Then I burst out, 'Stop spreading lies about me.'

Jake looked at me and just rolled his eyes contemptuously. It was this tiny gesture which so inflamed me again.

So then I surprised myself (and probably you too) by taking a punch at Jake. Don't start getting excited as it was a total disaster. My fist only brushed against his jaw in fact.

Still, a look of fury flashed across Jake's face. 'Why you—' he began. But he didn't finish that particular sentence. Instead he sent his fist crashing into my face with such a force I was sent reeling backwards. I crashed against the desks, just managing to stop myself from falling right on to the ground.

But I felt very strange. I was breathing in gulps and couldn't see properly. 'Don't pass out,' I said dizzily to myself. Around me was a sea of legs and shoes. And there was a lot of excited talking too, but I couldn't quite catch what was being said.

Then a new voice bellowed, 'What on earth is going on here?' I recognized that voice all right. It was Mr Leach — Leachy — the caretaker. A right busy-body, always sending pupils to his best pal, the Headteacher.

I peered blearily up at him. At the same moment I realized blood was gushing down my face. I scrambled about in my pocket for a hankie. Tim thrust one in my face. Leachy helped me to my feet, breathing stale coffee into my face as he demanded, 'Who did this to you?'

'I did,' muttered Jake. 'But he started it, didn't he?' He turned to the rest of the class. There were very faint murmurs of agreement.

'Right, well you'd better stay here,' said Leachy to Jake. 'The rest of you, go home now. You and your friend,' he pointed at Tim and me, 'follow me.'

He took us to the little sick room, near the Headteacher's office. Leachy got me to sit on the bed and pinch my nostrils while Tim held wet paper towels over my nose. The bleeding finally subsided, but I could still taste blood in my mouth and to tell the truth it isn't one of my favourite flavours.

Then the caretaker went off to talk to Jake.

Tim said to me, incredulously, 'But you never

get in fights.'

'Thought it might be a good time to start . . . Well, you saw how brilliant I was.' I smiled. Tim grinned too.

Then he went on, 'Jake shouldn't have grassed you up to Leachy.'

This was the very first time I'd ever heard Tim criticize Jake about anything.

Next moment the sick-room door swung open. The caretaker and Jake loomed in the doorway. And, to my total surprise, Jake smiled at me and declared, 'I'm here for peace talks.'

CHAPTER TEN

'I really think it's time you and I sorted out our differences,' went on Jake in this very reasonable tone, 'don't you?'

My heart thumped. Had my feeble punch achieved something after all? Had it brought Jake to his senses at last?

'Yes I do,' I said.

Leachy nodded approvingly. 'We'll leave you two to make up while I go and tidy up the classroom. You can help me,' he said to Tim. 'And,' he waved a fat finger at me, 'fighting solves nothing.'

Before leaving, Tim hissed, 'It'd be so brilliant if you and Jake can make up.'

Jake stood in front of me. 'Didn't mean to hit you that hard.'

'Didn't you?'

'So how are you?'

'I'll live.' Then I demanded, 'Why did you spread all those lies about me?'

Jake didn't answer.

'And why do you keep calling me Garth – that's so pathetic.'

Jake still didn't reply. He walked around the sick room. 'Not very big in here, is it? What would happen if five or six people fell ill at the same time, or if we had an epidemic?' He didn't wait for me to answer. Instead, he went on, 'You and I were mates once.'

'I remember,' I said, dryly.

'Good mates, too. We trusted each other, told each other private stuff.' He lowered his voice slightly. 'Remember when you told me how you speak to your dead grandad. Well, I'll never tell a living soul about that. You can totally trust me, because I've got principles . . . unlike you.'

'No,' I protested.

'When you saw my picture in the shed, that was private business too,' he hissed furiously. 'I specially asked you to keep that between us. And what happens: just two days later you're shooting your mouth off about it to anyone who wanted to listen. I was new at this school too. I could have gone under in an instant. But did you care? No, you mocked me and . . .'

'All right, Jake,' I interrupted, wearily. 'We can never be friends again now. But can't we at least make peace? That's what you said you wanted.'

'It is,' agreed Jake.

'Well, all I ask is that you leave me alone. Surely you can do that . . . please?' I was begging now, acting as if Jake were some mighty Roman emperor and I was a lowly prisoner desperate not to be thrown to the lions.

Jake stared at me, considering.

'Please.' I was practically on my knees to him now. And he knew it.

A little smile crossed his face. He was really savoring his power over me. Then he looked grave again. 'Sorry,' he said, 'but I don't know what you might do.'

'I won't do anything,' I cried.

'The trust has gone and it can never come back,' said Jake solemnly. 'Just remember, you destroyed it. This is all your fault, not mine.' All at once his voice was chillingly quiet. 'We can't both stay at this school. One of us will have to leave for good. Well, I'm popular here. You're not.'

'Thanks to you,' I cried.

Jake went on in the same, whispery voice. 'There's a perfectly good school in the town called Westbury. Other kids from the village go there. You will join them. Talk to your mum about it tonight.'

'But I don't want to leave here,' I protested.

'Don't you really, Garth?' said Jake.

'Stop calling me that,' I cried.

'I'll call you what I like,' replied Jake, 'and you can't do a thing about it.' He gave me a large gloating smile. 'I bet you're sorry you betrayed me now. I'm teaching you a very hard lesson, aren't I?' He made as if to leave, then veered back. 'I'm not so funny now, am I, Garth?' he hissed.

CHAPTER ELEVEN

Tim's mum gave Jake and me a lift home. She maintained a diplomatic silence about our fight (if you can even call it that) as she thought things were now sorted out between us. So did Tim, who kept grinning at me.

Jake was also in really good spirits and did most of the talking. As I left the car Jake said to me, 'Good luck, Garth,' as if I were leaving for good. Then he smiled. How desperately I wanted to punch that smile into the middle of next week.

Sitting on the front wall of my house was Lisa. Since she's turned sixteen she's been really acting up, arguing with Mum about everything. She's also got herself a boyfriend: you know the sort, all moody stubble and pouty lips. She had her arm around him now. 'Hi Lisa,' I said, just to be polite. And do you know what she did? She flicked her hair about and snapped, rudely, 'Do I know you?'

Normally I'd have just laughed. But today it was the final straw and I yelled, 'Oh, why don't you go to hell,' and tore off inside.

Mum wasn't home yet. So I stomped straight upstairs. All that anger and frustration that I'd been bottling up suddenly came bursting out. Just who did Jake think he was, telling me to leave my school that I'd gone to for two and a half years.

What was it he'd said? *'I'm teaching you a very hard lesson.'* The arrogance of him. If only I could . . . what . . . ? What could I do? I paced furiously around the room. Jake had already turned the entire class against me and made my life a total misery. What chance did I have against him?

NONE! NONE! NONE!

In a blaze of frustration I started pounding my fist against the wall as hard as I could.

But my anger didn't subside. It grew stronger. It was like some great tornado whirling and raging about inside me which just had to be released. I started hurling my books on to the ground. And my CDs. And everything that was on my desk. They all came crashing down. Then I began kicking my wardrobe.

'*I'm teaching you a very hard lesson.*' Those words wouldn't leave my head. And every time I heard them I kicked my wardrobe even harder. I wanted to smash it to pieces. I wanted to totally destroy it and everything else in my bedroom, too. A little part of me was watching myself in horror, squeaking . . . 'What on earth are you doing?' But the tornado inside me was making so much noise it drowned everything else out, until I heard my mum calling, 'What's going on up there?'

'None of your business,' I bellowed back at her. That wouldn't stop her though. She'd be up here any second with all her questions and probing. And I couldn't bear that. But I knew what I could do: barricade myself inside my bedroom.

I hastily pushed my bookcase right in front of the door. For good measure, I shoved Grandad's chair there too. That'll keep her away. Now no one could ever get at me again. And I'd be safe always.

I flung off my shoes and slipped under the covers of my bed. All I wanted now was to lie in this bed for ever. My anger was at last ebbing away but I didn't feel calm and peaceful — just totally, totally defeated.

'Gareth.'

I snapped my eyes shut.

She tried to open the door then, when she couldn't, made puzzled exclamations.

'Gareth,' her voice rising. 'What's going on?'

'Nothing,' I cried, raising the covers over my head. 'Just leave me alone.'

'Has something happened?'

'Can't hear you,' I murmured.

'Come on, love, let's talk.'

I didn't reply, just buried myself further under the covers.

Mum banged on the door again.

I ignored her.

Then Lisa came pounding up the stairs. I heard Mum whispering to her, then asking, 'Do you have any idea why Gareth's so upset?'

'Actually, I think I might,' said Lisa.

That gave me a start. Had she heard what had happened at school today? But then she said, in this loud, piercing whisper, 'I think I've really upset him.'

She and Mum went downstairs then, so I couldn't hear any more. They'd probably gone into a huddle in the kitchen.

Did Lisa actually think her little crack had upset me so much? I nearly burst out laughing. About three or four minutes went by, then footsteps came up the stairs again and I heard Lisa whisper through the door, in a gentle voice (totally different to her usual one), 'Hello Gareth.'

I didn't reply.

She went on, 'I just wanted to say I'm really sorry for what I said to you outside. I never meant to upset you. It was only a joke, that's all.'

So Lisa was apologizing to me! I couldn't remember the last time she'd done that. It's quite nice being apologized to, actually. And normally I'd have left it there. But today I wanted my sister to suffer a bit more.

'You shamed me,' I cried. 'And I can't forgive what you said.' Then, with a shiver, I realized I was saying back to her words Jake had once used to me.

But Lisa had had enough of apologizing now. I heard her say to Mum, in her normal tone, 'Oh, he's totally over-reacting.'

Mum started trying to push the door open. 'Come on, help me Gareth,' she puffed.

I couldn't let Mum try and force my door open. She might do herself an injury. So I called out, 'All right, I'll open up.'

Sighing heavily, I got out of bed and pulled back the bookcase and chair, just enough for Mum to be able to squeeze inside. Then I quickly hopped back into the sanctuary of my bed.

Mum immediately started scrutinizing me while Lisa hovered uneasily in the background.

'You've had a nosebleed,' she cried.

'Yeah, it happened at the end of school.'

'Quite a nasty one too,' said Mum, studying my face intently. You'll notice it didn't enter Mum's head for a second that I might have been in a fight. It just wasn't something I went in for. She sat down on the bed. 'Lisa didn't mean those things she said to you, did you love?'

'I've already told him that,' snapped Lisa.

'So how about coming downstairs and having something to eat?' asked Mum.

I turned over in bed. 'I'm not hungry and I want to stay here.' Then I put my fingers in my ears. Yes, all right, I know I was acting like a sulky little wuss. But right then I just couldn't do anything else.

'We'll talk later, then,' said Mum, giving me a little pat on the shoulder. She and Lisa left together. But a few minutes later Lisa returned, carrying two CDs I'd wanted to borrow from her for ages. Without a word she flung them on the bed and left again.

Then Mum came back, this time with a tray of food. I just picked at it. 'Not hungry,' I said.

'Not hungry,' echoed Mum disbelievingly. 'But you're always starving.'

This was true.

'Not going off my cooking, are you?'

'Mum, I'm just not hungry today. It's no big deal,' I replied defensively.

'Of course it isn't. It's just you haven't seemed yourself lately. You're normally so bouncy.'

'You make me sound like a beach ball.'

Mum smiled. 'And if you're upset about something, well, I feel upset too.'

I rather liked Mum saying that. But I really didn't want her to start probing me about what was wrong. That would have been too embarrassing. One day soon, I'd have to ask her about changing schools. But not tonight.

So I twisted my face into a smile and said, 'I just felt a bit fed-up earlier, but I'm over it now and I'm OK. Honestly.'

Mum glanced down at all my books and CDs littering the floor. 'And don't worry, I'll pick them all up,' I said.

'I'm not worried,' said Mum. 'We all get a bit fed-up sometimes and want to throw things about, it's no big deal.' Then she added unexpectedly. 'If ever you want to have a friend round . . . I'll stay right out of the way as well. I'll just leave a tray of food by the door and I won't do anything embarrassing.'

'You're not embarrassing,' I said.

Mum flushed a little with pleasure, then said softly, 'I do worry about you being on your own so much.'

I just muttered, 'Well, stop worrying, I like being on my own.' But what I didn't tell Mum – although I'll tell you – is that I really wasn't sure if I was on my own any more. I had a feeling Grandad had come back.

I'd certainly sensed him close by several times.

Also Grandad always wore this very sweet-smelling soap. And last night when I woke up I could smell it really strongly. That had cheered me up no end.

Did Grandad know I was in trouble? Was he keeping an eye on me? I hoped that was true. More than anything, though, I needed to talk to him.

So that night I took down Grandad's Avenger mask and, concentrating as hard as I could, said, 'Grandad, I think you're haunting me. Well, I'm just so happy about that and not scared at all. But please come back properly. I need to talk to you urgently. You're my only hope.'

Then I lay in bed, absolutely certain Grandad would pick up my S.O.S. and appear. I waited for ages. But nothing happened until another voice oozed its way into my room: *'I'm teaching you a very hard lesson.'*

I tossed and turned in bed, but Jake's horrible whispery voice wouldn't leave me alone. It even snaked its way into my dreams. *'I'm not so funny now, am I, Garth?'* Jake whispered right down my ear.

'Go away!' I yelled, and woke myself up.

I looked around. The dark was at its deepest now, yet I liked it that way. I found it oddly protective. If only it would stay dark and I could remain hidden beneath it, safe and secure.

But soon light would splash on to the curtains. And I'll know another day is creeping up on me. Funny how it's the daylight I fear. That makes me sound like a vampire. I smiled briefly at that. But then I thought of another day at school and tears started to creep down my face.

What was I to do?

There really was only one way out. I'd have to change schools. That would mean Jake had won, of course. But I felt as if I had nothing else left inside me now.

Surrender was the only answer.

And then, quite suddenly, a wave of Grandad's sweetly scented soap filled the air, just as it had last night. Only it was even stronger tonight.

All at once the rocking-chair started to creak as if someone was settling down on it.

Just when I'd given up all hope – Grandad!

I reached out to switch on the light, but a voice said, 'No, don't switch on the light.'

Had someone actually spoken aloud – or had I just heard it in my head? I really wasn't sure.

'Grandad, did you just speak to me?' I whispered.

I peered into the darkness. And then the breath caught in my throat.

I could make out a figure sitting in the rocking-chair.

But it wasn't Grandad.

CHAPTER TWELVE

This was someone much younger than Grandad. I could tell that by the way he was moving. He appeared to have some sort of cape around his shoulders, while on his face was . . . my heart started hammering away inside me . . . a mask.

I leaned forward.

A mask with – white lines all across it.

'Avenger. It's Avenger,' I gasped, my voice fluttering about all over the place.

Then I heard a voice – Grandad's unmistakeable voice – asking, 'So you can see me?'

'Yes,' I kind of squeaked.

'Well, stone the crows, I've got through at last.'

Then Grandad laughed his deep, rumbly laugh while I just stared and stared at him.

'Now I'm not frightening you at all, am I?' he asked, anxiously.

'Not at all,' I said, hastily. 'It's just you're . . .' I faltered.

'Oh, you can materialize at any age you want. So I thought I'd come back to you in my proudest days.'

Indeed, he could have stepped right out of that Avenger photograph in my bedroom.

'But is this real?' I asked, suddenly.

'I should jolly well hope so,' he said.

'I'm not dreaming then?' I murmured.

Grandad didn't answer. I looked across at him. I couldn't see through him as you're supposed to do with ghosts. He seemed completely solid. 'This is amazing,' I cried. 'I can't believe it. I've brought you back, haven't I?'

Grandad nodded, then said, 'Against all the rules for us to be chatting like this, you know. I'm not sure how long you'll be able to see me for . . . I could conk out again at any minute.'

'Oh no,' I cried, disappointed.

'We'll just have to talk fast. Now I've heard everything you've said about Jake, including tonight's instalment.' He paused for a moment. 'Well, don't worry, I've seen off far worse opponents than him, you know.'

'But that was wrestling, Grandad.'

'Same principles apply.' He tapped his head. 'You've got to get the mindset right. If you don't, then it doesn't matter how much talent and skill you've got, you're lost. Not talking too quickly for you, am I?'

'Not at all.'

'When I wanted to be a top wrestler, everyone laughed. How dare a scrawny little guy like me have such dreams. So, do you know what I did?'

'You used your mind.'

'Go to the top of the class. I studied my opponents at every chance I got and found out their weaknesses. Everyone's got some.'

'Not Jake,' I murmured.

'Of course he has,' cried Grandad, indignantly. 'I can smell a phoney. And I'll tell you, he's one for certain.'

I gaped at him.

'Now why did he never want you to talk to his parents? That's worth investigating for a start. So build up a dossier on him. Write down everything you can find out. You can never know too much about your enemy. Now, can you still see me?'

'Very clearly.'

'Good, because there's something else I've got to tell you that's very important. One day out of the ring I had to do something that I found very hard. In fact, I couldn't do it at all until I imagined that I was still wearing my Avenger mask. Then I took a deep breath, and as I was breathing out I said, "I am Avenger." I repeated this over and over. And suddenly I was just flooded with power, didn't feel like myself at all. And at last I was able to do this very difficult thing.'

He paused then said, firmly, 'You're about to discover the great power that is inside you.'

I made scoffing noises. 'You won't find much power inside me.'

'Oh yes we will, but only if you follow my instructions. Will you do that?'

'Yes, Grandad.'

'Good lad. Now I want you to close your eyes. Got them closed?'

'Yes.'

'Now imagine you're wearing my Avenger mask. I need you to fix that picture in your mind.'

I tried. But the trouble was, the picture kept slipping and I started thinking about something else.

'Not easy, is it?'

'No,' I admitted.

'Nothing important ever is. Come on now, I want you to really stretch your imagination. Start visualizing yourself in my mask . . .'

At last an image did begin forming. 'I think I've got it,' I said.

'Excellent,' said Grandad. 'I want you now to feel that mask about your face. Maybe it tickles slightly?'

'It does,' I said.

'Now, take a deep breath and say, "I am Avenger."'

'I am Avenger,' I muttered.

'No, no,' cried Grandad. 'Say it as if you mean it. Come on.'

'I am Avenger!' I shouted at him and opened my eyes.

'A bit better,' said Grandad. 'I want the first words you say when you wake up in the morning to be: "I am Avenger." And as you're walking to school repeat it over and over . . . then go and tell your teacher you are entering the talent show after all.'

'What!'

'Will you do that?'

I nodded.

'Say "I am Avenger" often enough, and those words will put a spell on you.'

'Oh, not a spell.' I said disbelievingly.

Grandad smiled deep into my eyes. 'You've got to trust me on this one.'

'All right,' I repeated. Then we grinned at each other.

'Any other instructions, Coach?' I asked.

'Yes, Jake may have knocked you out in Round One. But remember, Round Two starts tomorrow.

So get back on your feet – and never forget you're armed with magic now. And remember, too,' said Grandad, 'I'll be close by even if you can't see me. I'll be there.'

I was going to reply, 'That's good to know,' but I was asleep before I could say anything.

I didn't wake up until Mum drew back the curtains.

'Time to get up, I'm afraid,' she said.

'I am Avenger,' I murmured, then I smiled at her.

'Now, you seem more cheerful this morning,' she said.

Well of course I was, because the most wonderful, brilliant thing had happened. Grandad was back with me. And with his coaching, I felt as if I could face any opponent – even Jake.

CHAPTER THIRTEEN

That morning, Web-Head saw Jake and me on our own. She wanted to know why we'd started fighting in her classroom.

Jake replied, in this annoyingly reasonable voice, 'Well, I was having a party but I didn't invite Gareth. He got rather upset about that and started fighting me.'

That made me sound totally wet, didn't it? No wonder Web-Head gave me an odd look. She asked me if I wanted to add anything but I just murmured, 'No.' How could I explain why I'd really fought Jake?

She said, 'I can understand how horrible it is to be missed out from a party. Especially as you used to be such good friends, didn't you?'

Jake nodded gravely.

'But fighting really isn't the answer.' Web-Head was eyeballing me now.

'You might like to know, Mrs Webber,' said Jake, 'that I told my parents what had happened – and they were so angry they made me cancel my party for Alice on Friday night.'

'Oh dear,' murmured Web-Head, 'but I can understand why your parents decided that.'

'So can I,' said Jake. 'And next time someone attacks me I won't fight back. I'll tell a teacher.'

He was so slimy and crawly to her Web-Head just lapped it up.

Then I remembered what Grandad had told me to do today.

'Is it too late to enter the talent show?' I asked.

'I'm afraid the closing date was yesterday.' But then she added, 'I'm sure we can squeeze you in, though. Actually, I was very surprised you didn't enter before. So, good luck, Gareth.'

I noticed Jake's mouth tighten. But he couldn't say anything in front of Web-Head.

There was widespread disappointment when the class heard Jake's party had been cancelled. I thought they might have blamed me. But instead they were fairly suspicious, saying things like, 'Your parents cancelled a party because of one punch?'

To which Jake replied, 'Oh yes, they're incredibly strict.'

Then someone else asked, 'But how did they know about the fight?'

'The caretaker rang up my house, didn't he?' said Jake. 'Went on about it for ages to my old dear.'

I thought that was a bit strange as Leachy hadn't called my house at all.

Tim wasn't the only one to notice, either, how speedily Jake had grassed me up to the caretaker. For the first time since he'd arrived here, Jake had a bit of a difficult time.

He spent most of lunch-time on his mobile phones. Then, in the afternoon, he announced he'd managed to get five tickets to a film premiere. He'd better save one for Alice, he said with a stupid leer, and he couldn't forget his mate, Tim. But there were two left over, was anyone interested? Of course everyone was. And Jake was back firmly in control again.

Later that afternoon something rather odd happened. I was getting a few things for Mum at the local shops when I walked straight into Jake's mum.

'Oh, sorry,' I began. Then I recognized who she was and felt my face redden. I thought she might start giving me a lecture about fighting. Instead, she was smiling at me and saying, 'It's Gareth, isn't it . . . ? We haven't seen you lately.'

'No,' I replied doubtfully. Surely she knew why.

'Well I hope to see you again soon. Bye for now.'

I stared at her. She was supposed to be so furious about my fighting with Jake that she'd cancelled a party. Well, she didn't seem very irate to me. In fact she couldn't have been friendlier.

I wondered, suddenly, if Jake had ever really intended having a party for Alice at all. Especially as he was so funny about anyone going inside his house.

Maybe he just said that to show off. So how convenient that he and I had that fight. That gave him the perfect opportunity to cancel the party that never was.

And what about this film premiere? Would tickets for that ever actually materialize? Or was it just another of his promises? And who exactly did he talk to on his mobiles anyway?

I jotted all these thoughts down in my Jake dossier, just as Grandad had suggested. Then I waited for it to get really dark and for my room to come alive again. It was like waiting for Christmas Day to start.

But there was no sign of Grandad for ages, although I sensed he was here. I told him all that had happened that day, after which I drifted off to sleep. A voice woke me up. Someone was saying my name.

I opened my eyes to see Grandad standing by the end of my bed. Like last night, he had come as Avenger.

'What a good start you have made,' he declared.

'You heard me then?'

'I certainly did. Now, from tomorrow, I want you to start practising all your impressions.'

'Yes, sir.'

'And how many times have you said, "I am Avenger" today?'

'Oh, hundreds.'

'Is that all?' cried Grandad in mock indignation. 'Say it a thousand times tomorrow.'

'A thousand!'

'At least. And each time picture yourself wearing this Avenger mask. Then let those words fill your mind, and really see yourself as this figure of awesome might and then . . .'

'Yes?' I said, eagerly.

'Then things will really start to happen. And that's a promise.'

CHAPTER FOURTEEN

Every evening I practised my impressions. And on the night before the talent show I gave Mum and Lisa a preview. Even Lisa laughed – and she only laughs about twice a year.

The following morning all the pupils in Years Four, Five and Six trooped into the school hall for the talent show contest – twenty-six of us settled in the front row. We were the contestants.

We watched the microphone being set up and four chairs placed opposite it. These were for the judges: two teachers, a parent-governor and a pupil.

And these judges had a special power. Although

each contestant was allowed three minutes, as time was tight, if one of the judges felt they'd heard enough, they could wave a red card. Two judges displaying red cards meant you had to sit down immediately.

The judges took their places; first the teachers, then Mrs Lee, the parent-governor (very gushy and gets excited about everything!), and finally, the pupil judge . . . JAKE.

He swaggered to his seat. He winked at Alice (it was rumoured he would be asking her out today), then he flashed me a small smile of triumph.

And I knew he'd volunteered to be a judge for just one reason: to sabotage my chances. I wondered if I should back out now, pretend to be ill or something.

In the end I decided against that. I got very nervous though. And when it was my turn, I stood up so suddenly I knocked my chair over.

That caused a few sniggers.

Web-Head, who was introducing everyone, told me to start. I opened my mouth. My throat had gone very dry. And my tongue was growing. It really was. I let out this strangled gasp.

'When you're ready, Gareth,' prompted Web-Head.

There were more sniggers.

My whole body was tingling with nerves now. I told myself to relax. But that just made me tense up even more. Finally, I stuttered into my first impression. But I did it really flatly and my timing was off. I'd done it so well for Mum and Lisa yesterday. And Mum had said it got my act off to a really strong beginning. Not today, though.

I glanced across at Jake. He'd picked up his red card already, and there was such a nasty smile hanging off his lips. If only he hadn't been there. I could have coped with him in the audience, but not as a judge.

Seeing him so close kept reminding me of the last time I'd done some impressions for my class. And not one person had even smiled. I couldn't stop thinking about that.

And Jake was waving his red card about as if it were a flag now.

Then I saw Mrs Lee's hand hovering over her red card too. Any second now I was going to be sent off. Oh, the shame and humiliation. Grandad was going to be so disappointed in me.

Suddenly, into my head flashed Grandad telling me to: 'Visualize yourself in the Avenger mask.'

I closed my eyes, imagined myself in that brilliant, protective mask and said, very slowly, 'I am Avenger.' Just saying those three words seemed to kick me forward. And I burst into my next impression of Web-Head.

I've impersonated her so many times, but never as well as I did it that day. The whole audience seemed to suddenly come to life ... and I thought, Grandad was right. Saying those words had put me under a spell. I could do anything now.

I roared through the rest of my act. The audience started to whistle their approval. And by the time I'd finished I got a massive cheer which just went on and on.

I stood there, breathing in great, big bursts. I knew I wouldn't be chosen, not with Jake on the panel. But at least I hadn't let myself down.

After we'd finished the judges went into a huddle. I could hear them whispering away, especially Mrs Lee. Then she stood up and announced the names of the three winners. One from each Year. And the Year Six winner ... was me.

I just couldn't believe it. Afterwards the three of us went up to be congratulated by the panel. 'Your nerves got the better of you at first, didn't they?' cooed Mrs Lee to me, 'but then you just seemed to find your confidence.'

I nodded.

'And then there was no stopping you.' She leaned forward, confidingly. 'I was determined you should be one of our winners.'

'Thanks very much.'

I looked at Jake. He was sitting next to Mrs Lee and pretending to be studying his notes.

'And thank you so much, Jake,' I said.

He looked as if I'd just bitten him.

Then Tim came over. 'Everyone's talking about your impressions. They reckon you should be on the telly.'

I smiled modestly. Jake got up. 'Meet you outside,' he said crisply to Tim.

I thought he was going to walk right past me, but instead he said, in that nasty, whispery voice which he seemed to reserve just for me, 'You can never escape from my revenge.' The words themselves – and the way he said them – made my skin prickle with fear and all my pleasure at winning a prize at the talent show just drained away.

In the afternoon, my pencil-case went missing. I knew at once that Jake had taken it. And I thought, all that dramatic, spooky warning in the morning about never escaping his revenge, and what does he end up doing — stealing my pencil-case. How pathetic is that? And how typical of Jake. He was just a big talker, nothing else.

For the first time he really didn't scare me.

CHAPTER FIFTEEN

After tea on Friday, Mum left Lisa and me on our own. She was going off to a big writers' conference (although Mum works in a building society, she's also had some articles published: one about how it was better for women to stay un-married than settle for second best got reprinted masses of times and paid for my new computer).

Lisa also set off that evening to go to a party; she'd promised Mum faithfully that she'd be home by eleven o'clock. And Mum had believed her! Of course, I didn't.

I wasn't at all surprised when a very giggly Lisa rang up to say it would be difficult to get home, because . . . but I won't bore you with everything else she said. She certainly didn't want Mum to know she'd messed up – even offered me a fiver to say nothing. Any way, I was home alone, which I didn't mind at all.

I told Grandad all about the talent competition and, although I couldn't see him, I knew he was listening. Later I tried to go to sleep but the wind kept disturbing me, howling and whining outside like a dog begging to be let in. Every so often it would let out a great wail of fury and hurl itself at my window.

Then, just as I was drifting off, a new sound from outside made me jump awake. A soft, metallic chink. I knew at once what it was. Someone was easing open the latch on the back gate.

A burglar. He was trying to find his way into the house. Luckily I'd checked the doors before I'd gone to bed, and I knew they were all locked, so I was safe. I told myself that any burglar would soon discover he couldn't get in and move on to another house. But my heart still raced with fear.

I sat up, listening to nothing except my heart bumping away. And then I suddenly remembered something. Once before I'd heard the latch on the back gate open. Mum had been here then. And Lisa. And the three of us had crept downstairs only to discover a cat curled up on top of the back gate.

It could be that same cat now. And I was lying there, quaking in my boots, because of a mangy moggy.

In the end I scrambled out of bed and sneaked a look round the curtains. I saw a shadow moving off down the garden.

A human shadow.

Someone was out there all right. But what was he doing roaming about in the garden? There was nothing worth stealing – just a poky little shed with a leaking roof and hardly anything in it (none of us are gardeners).

I squinted outside. Everything was still again. There was that eerie hush you only hear at night.

Where had he gone?

Then into the silence came a sharp, pinging noise against my window. Something had just struck it.

The next thing I knew a whole volley of things began hitting the window. It sounded like gunfire. I felt as if my head was going to burst with shock.

What on earth was going on? And why would a burglar . . . ? Only it wasn't a burglar doing this, was it? It could only be . . . it had to be . . . JAKE.

He was furious about the way I'd acted at school today and this was his revenge. Up to today, he'd only picked on me at school but now, suddenly, he was attacking me at home in the dead of night. Nowhere was safe from him.

Did he know I was on my own? I had a horrible feeling he did. Maybe he'd been watching my house. That thought sent a shudder running through my body. What would he do next? Smash a window? Try to get in? He was clearly mad with rage.

I was cowering by my bed now, whimpering with fear. Telling myself I was acting like a baby, I quickly saw myself in the Avenger mask and rattled, 'I am Avenger' over and over. Only this time nothing happened and I didn't feel an atom braver. So it wasn't magic after all. This morning had just been a fluke.

CRACK!

Something hit the window with real force. Oh, why wasn't someone else here? Even if it was just my sister. I sank down on the carpet. Jake had really thrown me off balance this time.

I closed my eyes.

'Grandad,' I hissed, 'saying "I am Avenger" hasn't worked. And I'm really scared. Please help me.'

Almost at once the air went very chilly and a sweet soapy smell rushed into my nostrils. I felt a prickle of excitement.

Then out of the darkness I saw a smudge of grey smoke streaming towards me. Suddenly it stopped, grew much thicker and then started swirling and circling about. A shape seemed to be gathering, forming, moving. I wasn't the least bit alarmed, as I knew it was Grandad struggling to come alive again.

The shape gave a quiver and disappeared into

the dim smoke again and I heard Grandad's voice. 'Am I through yet?'

'I can hear you all right,' I said, 'but I can't see you.'

'Oh, what a confounded nuisance,' cried Grandad. 'Still, I never was a pretty sight.' Out of the ghostly haze came Grandad's unmistakeable laugh. 'Well, at least you know I'm here, don't you?'

Before I could reply a further assault of firing made me nearly jump out of my skin.

'Opponents used to do the same to me, you know,' said Grandad calmly.

'Throw stones?' I cried.

'No, but they'd try and rattle me just like he's doing at the moment. What you've got to do, Gareth, is get up and pull those curtains right back and face him . . . Do it now.'

'Not sure I can,' I replied apologetically. 'I did try saying "I am Avenger" but it let me down this time.'

'Say it again,' urged Grandad, 'but this time say it as if you really believe it. Picture yourself as that mighty costumed figure . . . and don't gabble the words. Let them settle inside your head . . . Will you do that for me?'

'Yes, Grandad,' I said softly. I walked over to

the window, saying each word carefully and imagining I was wearing that wonderful mask. I had to say 'I am Avenger' three times before the magic kicked in. Then all at once I felt this warmth surging all through my body.

'I am Avenger!' I cried out one more time. A feeling of great strength was rushing through me now. It was just so intoxicating. I strode over to the curtains and yanked them right back. Something else landed with a thump against the glass. And I recognized it as . . . my pencil-case. All those things I'd heard smacking against my window earlier must have been my pens and pencils and rubbers.

Then I saw Jake, silhouetted against the branches of the old oak tree in the middle of the garden. He was crouched on one of the branches like a gigantic bird of prey. But shall I tell you something: as soon as I could see him he seemed, all at once, far less frightening. He suddenly noticed me standing there and sent some pens whizzing at the window. Some stones, too. Only this time I didn't even flinch.

Then I saw him climb quickly down the tree and dart across the garden. The gate came briefly to life once more and there was silence again.

I let out a great sigh of relief. Tonight's raid was over.

'He's gone, Grandad,' I said. 'We've seen him off.'

There was no answer.

I turned round.

Grandad had vanished again. But the scent of his soap lingered, proving he had been here and I hadn't just imagined it.

I didn't sleep well at all. As soon as it was light I got dressed and went out to the back garden.

My pens and pencils lay scattered across the grass like the victims of a war. And I noticed something hanging off the branches of the oak tree.

It was a prospectus for Westbury School.

CHAPTER SIXTEEN

Later that morning Lisa rang. She started telling me how she still couldn't get home (went into this long, boring explanation) but I mustn't 'breathe a word to Mum about any of this if I wanted to keep the fiver . . .' then she suddenly exclaimed, 'You sound awful.'

'Oh, thanks.'

'You are all right?'

'Of course I am.'

'Missing me, aren't you?' she teased.

'Every second,' I replied, sarcastically.

But actually, I would have been embarrassingly pleased to see my sister that day. I just didn't want to be on my own any more. Jake's late-night assault had unnerved me. And I kept wondering if he would strike again.

I wasn't really hungry, so I just had some cereal for lunch, watched a few dire cartoons then dozed upstairs on my bed for a few minutes — or so I thought.

A blood-curdling wail woke me up.

My eyes sprang open. My bedroom was wrapped in darkness. I must have been asleep for hours and hours. Then I heard someone rattling madly on the door.

Jake.

His name shivered in my head. What was he up to now? 'I am Avenger,' I said, slowly. And I've got to face him, haven't I, Grandad? I can't hide away.'

I slipped out of bed and happened to glance at my Avenger mask. It was moving. Only very gently. Just as if it were being blown about by a small breeze.

And all at once, I just knew Grandad was telling me to wear it. I picked it up carefully. It was so precious I hardly ever put it on. But I was certain this was what Grandad wanted me to do now. So I did. It fitted pretty well too. I peered through the eye-holes. 'Now, I really am Avenger,' I said.

The door rattled again.

I charged downstairs, opened the front door and demanded, 'What do you want?' Only I said it in this deep, gravelly voice with just a hint of Count Dracula. Don't ask me where it came from, but it was dead spooky. Even scared me a bit.

All at once I realized the person banging on my door wasn't Jake at all. Instead I was looking at three people in masks. 'Trick or treat,' quavered one boy, staring at me very apprehensively.

Of course, it was Halloween tonight.

'Oh, right,' I muttered in my normal voice, darted off, found some chocolates, and handed them round. I recognized the boys now. They were in the year below me at school. And we all started to relax. 'That's a great mask,' said one of the boys. 'I've never seen one like that before.'

'No, it's one of a kind,' I said proudly.

'Belonged to my grandad.'

After they'd gone I wondered how on earth I could have forgotten Halloween. One of my favourite days of the year. I'd gone trick-or-treating with Grandad last year. We had such a laugh too.

Felt a bit of a pang remembering that. But then I thought, why shouldn't I go out anyway? After all, I was wearing a brilliant mask. And it wasn't anywhere near as late as I'd first thought – only half past five in fact. I wouldn't ring on door bells or anything – I'd just soak up the atmosphere.

It was so cold outside it made my cheeks tingle. But my village was still crawling with kids in spooky masks and costumes. Some can't have been more than about four days old. No, honestly, there were some really little kids scampering about.

The night smelt of bonfires too, as over on the common there was a big Guy Fawkes party. Every so often the drab night would explode with fire-balls and shooting stars fizzing, hissing and crackling across the sky.

Everything was transformed that night. Even the boring old houses which I'd passed a million times before tonight had hairy vampire bats fluttering in the windows or, outside the front doors, pumpkins with smiles nearly as insincere as one of Jake's.

I really expected to see Jake marching about with his band of followers, but very happily I didn't.

I saw Alice, though.

Down this alleyway I heard someone – a girl – shouting, 'But why did you choose to go to such a rubbish school? Our school's got a much better reputation. We get some of the best exam results in the country, while your school . . .'

A whole babble of voices joined in now. I edged nearer. Alice was standing in the middle of all this, eyes cast downwards, saying nothing. Then she tried to leave, but they wouldn't let her. They were getting more and more worked up.

They all went to Westbury School, whose prospectus Jake had kindly deposited in my garden. There was rivalry between the two schools which occasionally flared up into something quite nasty. This looked like one of those moments.

I should do something, rescue Alice somehow. Or at least back her up. 'I am Avenger,' I said to myself. And at that moment, an idea hit me.

I stepped back into the dusty shadows so as little of my body as possible was visible — just the Avenger mask. Then I rumbled, 'Leave her alone. Let her go now.' And my voice was even scarier than before. It was just brilliant in fact, if I say so myself.

They all stopped talking and stood gawping at me in some alarm. Alice, seizing her chance, bolted off in my direction.

'Follow me,' I hissed. And she did. We both tumbled down that alleyway and out into the street.

'Are they following us?' she asked (I liked that 'us' just as if we were a team).

I glanced back. 'No, we're all right,' I said, still talking in my Avenger voice.

'They were getting really nasty so I don't know what I'd have done if you hadn't turned up.' She smiled gratefully at me.

Now I felt like a proper superhero. 'You're very welcome,' I said graciously.

'Are you . . .?' she began.

'I am Avenger,' I said firmly, keen to stay in this guise for the moment anyhow.

'Oh, right, I see.' She was standing under the orange streetlight now. A little smile crept over her face, but it wasn't a horrible one. Not at all.

'Are you going to a Halloween party?' she asked.

'Er, maybe,' I replied. 'Are you?'

'No, I've just been for a little walk . . .' Then, as if she felt she needed to say more, she added, 'My step-dad's idea of acting like a family is to have a go at me. My mum joined in and I just ran out of the house . . . stupid, really.'

'I don't think so,' I rumbled, my voice getting deeper every time I spoke.

'Well, thank you, Avenger.' She smiled at me again!

I thought, she's all right and then . . . well, I went a bit crazy, didn't I, and blurted out, 'Don't go out with Jake. He's not what he seems, you know.'

She looked totally astonished.

Covered in embarrassment now, I muttered, 'Anyway, got to go or I'll be late for . . . for . . . it,' I concluded lamely, and took off.

On the way home I suddenly remembered something else: I'd said all that stuff about Jake in my normal voice.

So if she hadn't guessed my secret identity before, she certainly had now.

CHAPTER SEVENTEEN

I wasn't very surprised when Alice totally ignored me at school on Monday. Especially after I'd found out the big news about Jake and her. In town on Saturday morning he'd asked her out and she'd said 'Yes please' or something like that.

Felt as if I'd made a bit of a show of myself with Alice now. But I'd also saved her from that gang. So she could at least have said 'hello' to me. It wouldn't have killed her to say one little word, would it?

Still, I didn't have to wait long to brood about that – as something else happened that day.

It started with Kieran actually. He came up

to me at break-time in the playground and demanded, 'Have you been saying you're too good for this school?'

'No, of course not.'

'And did you say this school is dragging you down?'

'Absolutely not.'

Kieran's face relaxed. 'I didn't think you'd shoot your mouth off like that. It just didn't sound like you. I suppose it was your mum's decision, was it?' Then before I could reply he started patting me on the back, 'No hard feelings. I know some of the guys there. They're not all idiots.'

I stared after him. What was he talking about?

Then Tim burst up to me. 'You can't leave,' he cried.

I gaped at him. 'Who said I'm leaving?'

'Everyone. The whole class is talking about it.'

That was a moment of nerve-tingling strangeness, I can tell you. But I swallowed hard and tried to keep my voice steady. 'Well, sorry to disappoint everyone but I'm not going anywhere.'

'Oh.' Tim looked relieved. 'There was a rumour going round that you'd been to Westbury and thought it was much better than here . . .'

'Wrong, wrong, wrong. You do believe me, don't you?'

Tim considered for just a moment. 'Yes, I do,' he said, quietly.

'Thanks,' I replied, equally quietly. 'Now, let me guess who's been spreading all these rumours: could it be Jake?'

'Actually I think it was him,' said Tim.

'I know it was,' I cried.

Tim leaned forward. 'Jake does make up things . . .' he began but then stopped, as Jake was sauntering towards us with several people from my class, including Alice.

'Just in case you're wondering,' I called out. 'I'm not leaving. That was all made up – by Jake.' There were murmurs of surprise. Alice, I noticed, didn't react – but avoided making any eye contact with me.

I hissed at Jake, 'So why have you been spreading rumours saying that I'm leaving?'

'Because you are,' replied Jake smoothly. 'You're going on Friday.'

'No I'm not,' I said.

The school bell rang. 'You lot all go inside,' Jake ordered. 'And Alice, tell Web-Head Garth and I will be in shortly.' He spoke as if he had the right to wander into lessons whenever he chose. Yet no one challenged him.

Soon it was just Jake and me in the playground.

'I'm not going,' I cried.

'Oh yes you are,' hissed Jake. 'I've decided.'

'*You've* decided.'

'That's right. I'll give you until Friday to sort things out.' Then he added, in this reasonable tone, 'I'm just putting you out of your misery. You can make a fresh start at your new school. But that's it, case closed. There's nothing else to be said.' His confidence was just breathtaking.

I gazed at him dazedly for a moment. Then I recovered myself and repeated, doggedly, 'I'm not going anywhere. Why should I?'

'Because,' hissed Jake, 'I'm sick of the sight of you.' He looked at me suddenly with so much venom I actually stepped back from him.

All this hatred because of a stupid impression. In that one moment, Jake changed from my mate to my deadliest enemy. And from that point on we were involved in some kind of duel, which only one of us could win.

'So what if I don't go?' I asked him.

'You really don't want to know.'

'Planning to throw some more pencils at my window, are you?'

'Oh, you really won't like what I've planned for you next,' whispered Jake.

He was bluffing, I told myself. But my heart still began to beat wildly.

Then, with a sneery smile, he said, 'Don't worry, I'll get you a card for Friday saying "Good Luck, Garth" and we'll all sign it.' He laughed at his own little joke and then strutted off to Web-Head's class as if he owned the whole school.

That night I wrote up what Tim had said in my Jake dossier. *'Jake does make up things.'* Those were his exact words. Tim was in rather a nervy mood for the rest of the day so it wasn't the right time to ask him any more. But I would find out what Tim meant by that later.

Grandad was right. There was something fake about Jake. If I could just nail exactly what that was . . .

The doorbell rang. A few seconds later Lisa came tearing up the stairs. As I hadn't told Mum about her weekend away, she'd been pretty friendly to me. But now she was positively twinkling, as she said, 'Someone to see you. Would you believe, it's a girl!'

CHAPTER EIGHTEEN

'What?' I gasped.

'Yeah. I was pretty amazed as well,' smiled Lisa, 'especially as she's quite pretty.' She winked at me.

'Is this some kind of joke?' I asked.

'Go and see for yourself,' she said, laughing.

I walked cautiously down the stairs and discovered Mum chatting in the hallway with . . . Alice.

I couldn't believe it. What was she, of all people, doing here?

Alice smiled nervously at me.

'I've come to borrow your history notes, just

like we'd arranged.'

I hadn't a clue what she was talking about but I went along with it. 'Oh, right.'

'And you promised to explain a few points, didn't you?'

'Yeah, sure,' I said, faintly.

'It's not often Gareth volunteers to do extra homework,' smiled my mum. She was obviously chuffed that a girl had come round to see me. But I was racking my brain. Why was Alice really here?

A thought struck me: had she brought a message from Jake? It would be just like him to use his girlfriend to catch me unawares.

Upstairs, in my bedroom, I said, 'You don't really want my history notes, do you?'

'Well, I wouldn't mind, actually, if you've got them handy.'

I dug out my history book. 'There you go.'

'Thanks.'

After which there was something of an awkward silence. Alice looked around her. 'What a nice bedroom . . . most boys' bedrooms smell of ponds. Well, my cousin's does anyway. But yours doesn't.' She smiled at me.

I gave her a wary smile in return. Just what was she up to?

She walked around my bedroom, stopping to pause at my photos of Grandad. 'He looks good fun.'

'Yes, he was.'

'Oh, is he dead now?'

I nodded.

'Oh . . .' Her voice fell away. 'I'm sorry.' She looked at the other photo: the one of Grandad as Avenger.

'Yeah, that's him too, in his wrestling days.' I picked up the Avenger mask which was on the bed beside me. 'And this is his very mask. The one I wore on Halloween. But you'd guessed that already.'

'Not at first,' she said. 'That voice you put on was superb, so scary.' Then she added, 'Do you mind if I sit down for a second?'

'No, I don't mind.' I watched her sit down on Grandad's chair. Then I said, 'I hear you're going out with Jake now.'

She looked away. 'Yes.'

'Congratulations,' I said, in the flattest voice you could imagine.

She looked up. 'Please don't say that, because I absolutely hate him.'

CHAPTER NINETEEN

Well, I hadn't been expecting Alice to say that at all. I was so stunned I was speechless for a couple of seconds. Then I asked, 'But if you hate him so much why are you going out with him?'

Alice squirmed in her chair. 'Because he's sort of blackmailing me.'

'What!'

'He came up to me in the town centre on Saturday and asked me out.' She sighed heavily. 'Now I know everyone acts as if he's some kind of celebrity and thinks he's the coolest person ever, but personally I find him a bit creepy.'

'Hooray,' I murmured.

'And besides, I'm not interested in going out with any boys at the moment. I like playing football with them but that's all. So I told him this. He went quiet for a bit and then he started talking about you.'

'Me!' I exclaimed.

'He said how you betrayed him but he'd got his revenge on you. And now you were the most unpopular boy in the school. He got all boastful, actually, said how he'd staked out your house on Friday, found out you were all on your own and launched a midnight raid. Is that right?'

'He threw stuff at my bedroom window, yes.'

'He was chuffed to bits about that . . . then he hinted that if I didn't go out with him he could do the same to me.'

I let out a whistle of shock and muttered, 'That's so totally out of order.'

'I know, but I panicked and said, yes, I would go out with him, but inside I was so angry and there was nobody I could talk to about any of this . . . except you. I didn't want to try and talk to you at school – not with Jake watching me like a hawk all the time.' She smiled nervously. 'So, here I am.'

I smiled back. 'You know Jake's told me to be out of the school by Friday or else.'

'He loves issuing his threats, doesn't he?'

'He was bad before but now he's just crazed with power. I'm amazed people don't realize that. It's as if he's put everyone under this spell.'

'But the bad magic can't reach us,' cried Alice.

'Only we two are immune,' I said.

We grinned shyly at each other. 'If only we could get everyone else to see what Jake's really like,' I said.

'Some of the girls did say they think Jake's big-headed and loves himself.'

'Well, that's something I suppose. But he's much worse than that. He's also a total liar.' I got up and showed her my Jake dossier. She read it avidly.

'This is great,' she said.

'But it's not enough. I've got to find out more about his life in London. That's what really gives him his cred at our school. Yet somehow he's got all these contacts who are always getting him tickets for film premieres. Well, I think he's exaggerated a lot of that. Maybe even made some of it up. That's why I'd love to chat with the two people Jake never wanted me to meet: his parents. I'm sure I could find out things from them.'

'Yes,' agreed Alice.

'If only I could think of some way of getting

inside Jake's house . . . it'll be very difficult . . .'

'But I could get in easily,' interrupted Alice, 'seeing as I'm supposed to be his girlfriend.'

I stared at her as she went on, eagerly, 'I could find out things in secret from his parents. Oh, I'd love to do that. Then I'd be paying him back and . . . helping you.' Her eyes shone as she asked me, 'So, come on, will you trust me with this assignment?'

I looked at her for a moment, then declared, 'As they say in the Sherlock Holmes film, "I shall put this case in your hands".'

CHAPTER TWENTY

It was so good knowing Grandad and I weren't on our own any more. We had an ally. A really top one, too.

Alice and I agreed not to talk at school. We didn't want to do anything to make Jake suspicious. But Alice decided to invite herself round to Jake's house the very next night. She rang me just before she left.

'Nervous then?' I asked.

'I'm shaking,' she replied, 'but it's exciting as well.'

'Just be very careful. If Jake suspects what you're doing . . .'

'I will never be seen again as Jake will have turned me into a bat . . .' We both started to laugh.

Then Alice said, 'By the way, I haven't told my mum a thing about Jake. She thinks I'm spending the evening round your house copying up more notes. So, if she rings up and wants to talk to me . . .'

'Yeah.'

'You'll just have to impersonate my voice.'

'Oh, great.'

'I'll come round and see you with a full report afterwards . . . wish me luck then.'

'I do, masses and masses of it.'

Waiting for Alice was just agony. To take my mind off things I did work on my impression of her. Couldn't get it, though. I didn't concentrate enough. I was too busy trying to picture what was going on at Jake's house. I hoped she wouldn't have to do anything grisly like kiss him.

Nine o'clock came, still no sign of her. She was staying at Jake's house a long time. Was that a good sign? Finally, just before half past nine the doorbell rang.

I was there, right away. Alice was out of breath. She spluttered, 'I've found out something you won't believe.' She stopped.

Mum appeared in the doorway, smiling questioningly at Alice. 'Alice needs some more history notes . . . really urgently,' I explained.

'So I see,' murmured Mum as Alice went gasping past her.

Upstairs, Alice fell onto Grandad's chair. I said, 'Tell me everything that happened. Omit no details.' (Which was another quote from Sherlock Holmes films, actually.)

'Well, I'd better talk fast as my mum will be ringing up any second . . .'

I nodded impatiently.

'Well, Jake opened the door and didn't look at all pleased to see me. In fact he asked me what I wanted, quite rudely. I said I just wanted to see him.'

'Ugh!'

'I know, but I had to make it convincing.'

'You didn't have to kiss him, did you?'

'Oh no, nothing like that. Jake and I just sat in

the sitting room. He mumbled a few things and stared at his hands a lot. He was totally different to how he is at school. And we sat watching TV – really boring. All the time I was looking out for his parents. His mum brought us in some tea, but there was no chance to talk then – especially as Jake got very tense when she was about. But then Jake went off to the loo and . . .'

'Yeah?' I said eagerly.

'I dived into the kitchen where his mum was doing some cooking. I took the tea-tray in and asked her what she was making. I thought I couldn't plunge in with questions right away. But then' – her voice started to rise now – 'I said to her, very casually, "I expect living here is very different to where you used to live before." And do you know what she replied?'

'No,' I practically screamed at her.

'She said, "Oh, not really. I just miss the sea, that's all . . ."' – she took a deep breath – 'Otherwise, life here isn't very different to that at Felixstowe.'

'What!' My head started to spin. I couldn't take in what she was saying. It was totally incredible.

'Well, I asked her where exactly Felixstowe was, and she said, "Oh, it's a lovely seaside town in Suffolk." And I asked if that was near London and she said, "Oh no, London is hundreds of miles away from Felixstowe." '

'So every single story Jake told us about life in London was made up!' I yelled.

'Of course they were,' Alice screeched back at me. 'He's never lived there at all!'

'It was all a pack of lies, every syllable of it,' I cried, still unable to take it in. The full extent of Jake's lying was shocking, terrible and awesome, all at once.

'I didn't get a chance to ask any more, as Jake came in then.'

'It doesn't matter. Hey, Alice, Sherlock Holmes would be envious of you tonight, you were magnificent.'

'We've got him, haven't we?' cried Alice, triumphantly.

'Oh yes, once the class find this out . . . well, this'll break Jake's spell over them all right. We've done it!' Those last three words came out as a shriek.

Mum opened the door. 'Is everything all right . . . ?'

'Yes, thanks.'

'You both sound very excited,' said Mum.

'We just love history, Mum,' I said, then added under my breath, 'especially Jake's history.'

After Mum had gone Alice asked, 'So what do we do now – announce this to the rest of the class?'

I nodded. 'We need to pick the right moment though.'

There was no time to say anything else as Alice's mum rang, demanded she return home at once.

But at break-time the following morning, Alice and I had a secret meeting. It was very brief as the last thing we wanted was for Jake to discover us together. We decided that we would announce the details of Jake's fake biography at lunch-time.

But unfortunately something happened to change all our plans . . .

CHAPTER TWENTY-ONE

It was a wet lunch-time that day, so we were allowed inside our classroom with one of the dinner ladies supervising us. As soon as everyone had finished eating, Alice and I planned to make our joint announcement about Jake.

Both of us were extremely nervous. I paced around the corridor while Alice played football in the classroom with a few of the boys. Strictly against the rules, of course. But the dinner lady was nowhere to be seen, so what did it matter? I could hear the boys cheering and shouting. Alice really was a good player.

Some more people from our class streamed back

from the dining room. I remember thinking, any second now we'll make our announcement.

But instead Alice completely missed her target, smashing a window into a thousand extremely noisy pieces. Everyone nearby — including me — pelted into the classroom. Poor Alice was staring at the broken window and declaring, 'My mum is going to kill me — and my step-dad. They'll absolutely kill me.'

'Not necessarily,' said a voice in the doorway: Jake. A few people shuffled away so he could take up his place in the centre of things.

Jake immediately took charge. 'We'll say a mad dog tore in here. It had red eyes and was dribbling saliva. It raced round and round the classroom. We think it had rabies. Then it jumped through the window . . .' People were listening to this tale, absolutely fascinated.

'Where's the dog now?' asked someone.

'He injured himself so badly he's dead, and we've buried him over there,' said Jake, pointing. I thought, you lie so easily, don't you. I suppose it's a kind of skill in a way.

Jake was really keen on this phantom dog story but in the end decided it might be easier if we just said we didn't see anything and none of us knew how the window got broken.

Then Web-Head was in the doorway, exclaiming, 'What on earth has happened here?'

'We don't know,' Jake said. 'We just found it like this, didn't we?' There were murmurs of agreement.

'What nonsense!' snapped Web-Head. She made us all sit down with our hands on our heads in silence – something she only does when she's really mad. 'Now, come on,' she said. 'Own up, the person who did this. At least have the courage to do that.'

Hard not to wilt beneath Web-Head's iron gaze. Alice was about to raise her hand when Jake shook his head vigorously at her. Mrs Webber pounced on him. 'Have you got something to tell us, Jake?'

'No, miss.'

Then her voice softened, because Jake was a favourite of hers. 'There are rules in this classroom and one of them is, we don't play football, isn't it, Jake?'

'Yes, miss.'

'And we all need rules, don't we?'

'Yes, miss,' he agreed again.

'So please tell me who broke our rule about football in the classroom.'

'Sorry, I don't know,' said Jake.

Web-Head's mouth tightened. 'All right, there

will be a class detention for one hour tomorrow'
– loud murmurs of protest - 'unless someone can
tell me by the end of school what has happened. I
shall be working in my classroom for half an hour
after school tonight. If the culprit isn't responsible
enough to come forward, I hope someone else in
this class is.'

No one said a word until the end of school, then
a great deal was said.

'Look, it's no good,' cried Alice to the group of
people around her. 'I can't expect you all to take
the blame for me . . . I'll just have to own up.'

'No, you won't,' said Jake, so firmly everyone
was silenced, just as if a teacher had spoken.
'Now, in this class we look out for each other. If
your mum finds out you've broken a window
she'll give you a real roasting. So we'll band
together and help you. That's what makes us a
diamond class. And that's why,' he raised a hand
as if to silence any further dissent, 'everyone is
going to stand by you, Alice.' Then he started
grinning triumphantly, like a proud salesman
who's just sold a really expensive car.

Alice smiled at everyone facing her. 'I don't
know what to say.' Her voice fell away. '. . . Just
so grateful.'

'In this class you're either for us,' Jake paused

and looked across at me, 'or against us.' Then he turned to Alice, 'Come on, I'll walk you home.'

They left together. Can't tell you how much I hated watching that.

Everyone else streamed off home, all talking about what had happened. To my surprise, a few were saying things like, 'It's not up to Jake to say what we're going to do.' And, 'Jake thinks he's in charge of all of us. Well, he's not.'

That cheered me up — a little. But I still couldn't help worrying if Jake had impressed Alice. Hard not to be a bit impressed, I suppose, when someone's just saved you from a major rollicking.

I sat thinking about all this in the library for a while. There was no one else about, which suited me fine.

As I left I bumped straight into Web-Head. 'Not gone home yet, Gareth?'

'I forgot something,' I explained. But Web-Head was still looking at me questioningly. She was wondering if I was here as a grass, wasn't she? Talk about insulting.

'Bye then,' I said and tore off.

I was just leaving when I spotted Jake of all people, slipping back into school. He was gazing about in a very furtive way too. I ducked out of sight, then followed him all the way to Web-Head's room.

I sneaked a glance at them through the window. They were both sitting down. Jake was spouting away and Mrs Webber was listening to him dead intently (but doesn't she always).

Had Jake slipped back here to grass up Alice? It was the most likely explanation, but even I couldn't quite believe Jake would do that. And to his girlfriend, of all people.

I drew closer to try and catch the odd word. Suddenly a hand grabbed my shoulder. I spun round to see Leachy, the caretaker, glaring suspiciously at me. He was always sneaking about.

'What are you doing here?' he demanded.

'Just looking for someone,' I stuttered.

'Who?'

'It's all right, they're not here.' Then I sprinted away.

I'd only been home a few seconds when Alice rang. 'I'm so sorry about what I did at lunch-time,' she whispered. 'I've ruined everything now, haven't I?'

'Of course you haven't.'

'Yes I have. Jake's taken charge again — and I suppose . . . well, he has helped me a bit.'

'I suppose,' I murmured.

Alice was waiting for me to say something else. And I nearly blurted out what I'd seen Jake do after school today. But then I thought — what if Alice started defending him and said I didn't know for certain what he'd been doing? I just couldn't bear that. So instead I decided to wait until next morning and see if my suspicions were confirmed.

At registration the next day, Web-Head came into the classroom with a very grave expression on her face. Then, with a real death rattle in her voice she said, 'Alice, I need to have a word with you please.'

Alice got up and rather than whisper together by Mrs Webber's desk, they went outside. A very bad sign. They didn't stand just outside the door either — they went off somewhere.

When Mrs Webber returned, she was alone. I immediately asked her where Alice was, but she just ignored my question. (Jake, by the way, didn't say a word.) Later, a girl who'd left for a music lesson came back and said she'd seen Alice facing the wall outside the Headteacher's office.

It was nearly break-time before Alice returned to our classroom. She kept her head down and looked very serious. Then I heard her whisper to a girl. 'Someone snitched on me after school to Web-Head.'

'Do you know who?' asked the girl.

'No,' said Alice. 'I don't.'

But of course, I did.

Every time I looked at Jake red-hot fury rushed through me. I was burning up with anger.

What a total hypocrite Jake was. After making all those big speeches he sneaks off and betrays Alice. Wasn't that just typical of him. I wanted to tell everyone right away what I'd seen. But something told me to wait just a bit longer.

Besides, I thought Alice had the right to know first.

So, after school I rang her. The Headteacher had already phoned Alice's mum. Her mum had gone ballistic, just as Alice had predicted. 'She said I'm grounded for a year,' cried Alice.

'She can't ground you for a year,' I said. 'That's against the law, isn't it?'

'Try telling my mum and step-dad that,' replied

Alice. 'They said I can't have any television, or PlayStation, or chocolates. I'll just be stuck in this house for a year eating vegetables.'

Then I told Alice who'd squealed on her.

She was silent for a moment, before saying slowly, 'You know when he was walking me home yesterday, he was too nice somehow . . . I felt as if he was putting it on.'

'I thought you'd be shocked.'

'At something Jake did? Never,' she said bitterly. 'So when he told me he'd left something behind at school . . .'

'He went tearing off to Web-Head, just as fast as he could,' I interrupted.

'Oh, I just can't wait to expose him,' cried Alice, 'and let people know about all the lies he's told . . . His whole life is just one, big, fat lie.'

It was right then an idea jumped into my head.

The best I'd ever had.

CHAPTER TWENTY-TWO

This was my idea.

I decided we needed to do something better than just stand up in the classroom and start spouting about Jake.

This was our one chance to land a knock-out blow on Jake, but we had to make it as dramatic as possible.

So I thought, why don't we make a tape called: *Jake: This Is Your Life*. It would be just like the TV shows, only we'd actually call it *This Is Your Lies* and tell all about Jake's fake life.

Alice got very excited when I told her about it. And we planned it all out that night on the phone.

Making the tape took me longer than I'd expected though, and it wasn't ready in the end until the following Monday. But I really wanted it to be perfect.

Over the weekend I took a chance and rang Tim — I told him I was making a tape, exposing all Jake's lies (I didn't give him any details) and did he have anything I could add to the list.

'How do you mean you're making a tape?' gasped Tim.

'It's a sort of *This Is Your Life*, which I'm calling *This Is Your Lies*.'

'You're going to play it in the classroom?'

'That's right.'

'Jake will go mad.'

'He won't be very happy, I know. But it's time to stand up to him.'

'Yes,' said Tim uncertainly.

'So have you got anything?' I asked for the second time.

All in a rush, Tim said, 'Well, you know he was supposed to be having a party at his house for Alice – and then his parents cancelled it because of him fighting with you.'

'Yes.'

'Well, I saw his parents just two days later, and I practically begged them to reconsider . . . but they just looked at me really blankly. Jake said they were furious with me for even asking them, but I don't think they had a clue what I was talking about.' He stopped. 'But you can't use that though.'

'Oh . . . why not?'

'Look, I'm sorry but I just don't think your idea is going to work.'

'What have I got to lose? According to Jake, I've left school anyway.' I stopped, but Tim didn't say anything so I said, 'It's OK, Tim, you needn't get involved.'

'No hard feelings?' Tim asked anxiously.

'None at all.'

'Jake has got very big-headed and the way he's treated you . . . I don't like it. But I can't . . .' He hesitated.

'It's all right. Just don't warn Jake what I'm doing.'

'As if I would.' Tim was highly indignant.

But I did have a little fear that Tim might say something to Jake.

On Monday morning I carefully packed my cassette-player. It didn't need plugging in. The tape was in, all set up.

I was early to school. So was Alice. We grinned nervously at each other but we didn't talk. Then Jake came swaggering into school. He spotted me and pretended to look astonished. 'I thought you'd left.'

'You thought wrong then, didn't you.'

Jake lowered his head and hissed, 'You're going to be very sorry you're still here. Very sorry.'

I didn't reply but I thought, that's going to be the very last time you ever threaten me.

The tables were about to be turned on Fake Jake.

CHAPTER TWENTY-THREE

Web-Head took the register to the accompaniment of my heart thumping away. When she'd finished, Alice stood up, just as we'd planned.

'Please, miss,' she wailed, 'can I talk to you?'

'Of course you can,' said Web-Head, waving her to the desk.

'No, no,' screeched Alice, 'it's personal.' I was highly impressed to see a few tears trickle down Alice's face too.

A very concerned Web-Head sprang up. 'All right, everyone, get on with your work. I'll only be outside. Come on, Alice.'

She put an arm around Alice and the two left

together. Her exit had created a buzz of interest. Now everyone was whispering about it, except Tim. He kept staring round at me.

So here it was. My chance. '*I am Avenger.*' The words came so naturally now, as if they were a part of me. Straightaway I could feel all this power brewing up inside me. I pulled out my cassette-player from my bag, strode up to the front of the class and plonked it down, then announced, 'This is something you should hear.'

'What is it?' asked Nicola.

'You'll hear in a second.'

Then the whole class heard my voice saying, 'Welcome everyone to a very special edition of — *This is your Lies.*' I was impersonating one of those cheery announcers whose voice positively hums with jolliness. 'And tonight, our subject is . . . *Jake.*'

In a flash, Jake was on his feet, bounding over to the cassette-player. 'We're not hearing this rubbish,' he announced, switching it off.

'Don't do that,' I cried.

'Yeah, put the tape back on,' called out Kieran.

There were loud cries of agreement. Jake stood there blinking rapidly. He was really shocked at this sudden outbreak of mutiny. But he also managed to smile and say, 'Well, I've got better things to do than listen to that garbage.'

He sat down again, picked up the book he had been reading and raised it until it was covering his face.

Meanwhile I switched the tape back on. I stared anxiously at the door, hoping that Alice could delay Web-Head for a couple more minutes at least.

On the tape I was saying, 'Well, here's your first lie, Jake, and it's a whopper.' And you could just sense everyone bubbling with anticipation as I paused briefly before declaring, 'You told every-one you came from London, but in fact you've never lived there in your life. Your parents told Alice you lived in Felixstowe for seven years before you came here. Isn't that right, Alice?'

'Yes it is.' This was my very bad impression of Alice (as she wasn't allowed out all weekend) but no one noticed that. They were too busy taking in that shocking information.

There were cries of, 'Is this true, Jake?' And 'Have you never lived in London?'

Jake didn't react, just sat there totally still, apparently completely absorbed in his book. But I could feel something happening to him.

The cassette whirred on and I was saying, 'Now, remember how Jake was always promising you tickets to premieres and . . .' But no one heard any more. Jake had suddenly erupted from his seat, picked up my cassette-player and hurled it on to the ground. The tape flew across the classroom. So did all the batteries and part of the back of my recorder.

'It's nothing but lies,' yelled Jake, 'from a bitter saddo.'

I shot to my feet too and called out, 'No, every word of it is true.'

We started squaring up to each other. Jake looked as if he was about to punch me again. But do you know, at that moment I really wasn't afraid. I was so fired up I felt capable of anything.

The door opened and Web-Head came striding back in, Alice behind her. 'What on earth's going on here? Can't I leave you reading quietly for two minutes? What is all this shouting about?'

Neither Jake nor I answered.

'I could hear you down the corridor,' continued Web-Head. Then she spotted the remains of my cassette-player. So did Alice who looked at me questioningly. I nodded towards Jake.

'And who does this belong to?' Web-Head snapped.

'Me,' I said.

'You know you're not supposed to bring tape-recorders into school, don't you, Gareth.'

'Yes, miss.'

'So why did you?'

'There was something I wanted everyone to hear.'

'During their reading time?'

'Yes, miss.'

She crouched down. 'So what's happened to it?'

'It fell off the desk,' I said. 'I must have put it too near the edge.'

Web-Head looked puzzled. 'So what was all the shouting about?'

'We were just annoyed we couldn't hear it all,' cut in Kieran.

Web-Head shook her head. 'That's why we tell you not to bring things into school, as they can get broken so easily. Well, you'd better pick up all the bits. You help him, Jake.'

So Jake and I crawled about on the floor. Actually, I collected everything up. Jake just slid this one battery in my direction.

Tim suddenly whispered to me, 'You did really well,' and clapped.

There were ripples of applause around the room until Web-Head declared, 'Stop this silly clapping. I don't know what's the matter with you all today.'

All through maths, people were whispering about what had happened. I sensed a gathering rebellion against Jake. People thought he'd betrayed himself when he threw my cassette-player onto the ground. To them, that was like an admission of guilt.

A note was passed to me from Kieran. He wanted to hear the rest of the tape at break-time on the back field.

So it seemed did just about everyone else.

Alice was late. Her performance had so moved Web-Head (Alice had pretended to be all distraught about the broken window, fearing it would tarnish her reputation at school) that she asked Alice to stay behind to talk some more.

And Jake didn't turn up at all. But the rest of my class was thronging about and so were masses of other pupils. By trying to trash my tape, Jake had actually ensured it played to a much bigger audience.

At first my player didn't work. But then Kieran discovered I hadn't put the batteries in properly and re-arranged them. The whole of Jake's *This Is Your Lies* was played again. And I held the player up in the air so that everyone could hear it more clearly.

They listened in stunned silence to the last part – about Jake, the grasser.

'So you actually saw Jake meet Web-Head after school?' said Gary.

I nodded. 'I watched him go right into her room and talk to her for several minutes.' Suddenly I felt as if I were a witness, giving evidence at a trial. Jake's trial.

Alice finally turned up and it was her turn to go onto the witness stand. 'Yes, his mum told me they'd lived by the seaside before they came here. They'd never lived in London.'

People were shocked all over again. Kieran suddenly patted me on the back. 'Jake's given you a hard time, hasn't he?'

It wasn't just Jake, I thought. He was the leader, but you all joined in. I didn't say anything though.

'Jake's been throwing his weight around here

for too long,' went on Kieran.

'Where is Jake?' asked Gary.

'Hiding,' called out someone else.

All at once we turned into a massive pack, determined to seek out Jake. He was quickly located sitting all by himself in our classroom. Not only my class, but hordes of other pupils swarmed round him.

'Why did you grass up Alice?' demanded Kieran.

'I don't know what you're talking about,' cried Jake. But there was something desperate in his voice now.

The questions rained down on him from every corner of the room.

'Why did you make up all those stories?'

'Have you actually met one famous person?'

Jake stared feverishly round at his army of accusers. 'Look,' he shrieked suddenly, 'if you believe Garth's lies, you're as twisted as he is.'

'It's not Garth, it's Gareth,' I cried, firmly. 'And you're the liar, not me.' My words were greeted with loud cheers. Several people, including Tim, patted me on the back.

The bell went. Jake got up and started pushing his way through all the people gathered round him. 'After all I've done for you,' he cried, half to himself. 'Well, I've finished with the lot of you.' When he reached the door, he said, under his breath, 'What do I care about you sweaty losers anyway?'

Before anyone could reply he'd stalked off down the corridor. Everyone was ready to pile after him but then Web-Head appeared and immediately started asking what all these people were doing in her classroom.

Jake didn't return to class and Web-Head suddenly noticed his absence. 'Where's Jake?' she asked.

Everyone stared blankly at her.

'Does anyone know where he is?' she demanded.

'He just walked out at the end of break, miss,' said Kieran.

'Did he say where he was going?'

'No,' replied Kieran.

'Oh dear.' She looked highly concerned. But then one of the school helpers – a large, rosy-cheeked lady who wheezed a lot – came in with a note for Web-Head.

She read it, then said, 'Ah, Jake's feeling unwell and he's in the medical room. There's a nasty bug going round, isn't there?'

'It's called Jake,' muttered a voice at the back.

Jake didn't reappear until the afternoon. Then

he just slunk in, not looking at anyone.

'Go to London, did you Jake?' hissed Gary. 'Or have you just grassed us all up?'

I'll never forget how Jake looked that afternoon.

I kept staring at him, unable to believe this was the enemy who'd cast such a long shadow over me these past few weeks. He looked as if he'd had all the breath knocked out of him. Now he sat crumpled in his chair like a dead balloon, crushed and defeated.

The second I got home I told Grandad what had happened. And later that night I saw him – but only very briefly, as I was dead tired.

I opened my eyes to see him standing by my bed. He was smiling. Then he jabbed his thumb in the air as a kind of victory salute.

'We did it, Grandad,' I mumbled, before falling asleep again.

CHAPTER TWENTY-FOUR

Next morning Tim was waiting outside the school for me.

'You were right,' he cried. I looked questioningly at him. 'About the tape. It was a brilliant idea.'

'Thanks.'

'And now you're the hero of the school.'

'Oh no.'

'Yes you are,' he said.

I smiled. 'From zero to hero in one day.'

'I could never ever have done what you did yesterday.' said Tim.

'Yes you could. You've just got to . . . well, see

yourself a bit differently.'

Tim looked away. 'Don't suppose you'd like to come round my house for tea tomorrow? he mumbled.

'Actually, I would,' I replied.

'That's excellent news,' cried Tim. And for a couple of seconds we just grinned at each other.

All day people congratulated Alice and me for exposing Jake. They went on to say things, like, 'Of course I was getting really sick of him posing about all the time,' and 'I knew there was something fishy about him. I never believed all his stories.'

'It looks like we needn't have bothered making that tape,' smiled Alice, 'as everyone had guessed what a phoney Jake was anyway.'

Jake himself didn't return to school for the next few days. Then, on Friday morning he was back. He stormed into the classroom, a mobile phone pinned to each ear, saying, 'Yeah, that's great. Fantastic. Owe you one, mate.' And he was strutting about the place as if nothing had happened.

I watched him alarmed and fearful. Was Jake somehow going to worm his way back again and regain his former status?

He strode over to Kieran. 'Hey, just been

chatting to my contact. I'll have that new football kit for you next week. Sorry about the delay, but it's all in hand now. You have my word on that, mate.'

Kieran looked at him, then said slowly, 'Do you really think I'm talking to you?' and turned right away from him.

Jake shrugged his shoulders and went over to another group of boys. 'I should also be able to get tickets for a big film premiere next month. It's a bit hush-hush which stars will be going . . .'

'Did you hear that voice?' interrupted one boy.

'No,' replied another boy. 'I didn't hear a thing.'

They blanked Jake completely.

Humming tunelessly to himself, Jake sat down, noticed where Tim was sitting (back next to me) but just carried on humming. At break-time he tried again, this time with the girls.

They just said, loudly, 'Don't say anything else, Web-Head's spy is listening,' and again totally ignored him, except for one of the girls who called out, loudly, 'Jake, just get over yourself.'

He then started chatting to some of the younger pupils. Only last week, they'd have been over-joyed if Jake had even looked in their direction. But they'd heard what had happened and so they blanked him as well.

This silent treatment didn't just last for a day or two. No, it went on and on and all the time new things were added to it.

So, one lunch-time, everyone decided they couldn't bear to even sit at the same table as Jake. They all squashed onto the other tables, to the great puzzlement of the dinner ladies.

'You're acting as if that poor boy has got the plague,' cried one dinner lady. That just made everyone laugh all the more.

Another day Jake walked on a step. Straightaway a boy yelled, 'I'm not walking on that, Jake's been there.' So he jumped over that step. So did his mates.

Perhaps all this sounds a bit cruel to you. But you've got to remember, everyone was very angry with Jake for tricking them so completely. And I think they were even angrier with themselves. They'd fallen for his act, hadn't they?

Jake didn't react to any of this. At lunch-time every day he took up his place right at the end of the table. And he affected not to notice the fact that no one ever spoke to him. After he'd finished eating he'd get up and start rushing around the school as if he were in a big hurry. Yet he never actually ended up anywhere. Then, after a while he must have got tired of doing that, because instead he sat right at the top of the back field all by himself. He didn't even try and be friendly now. If anyone came near him he'd give them a really fierce stare.

He finally stopped having lunch too. He just ate a few sandwiches on the back field, his eyes fixed all the time on the horizon. Then when the bell went he'd walk back into school, swinging his bag as he went, as if he'd just had the time of his life.

One lunch-time Alice and I observed him in his usual habitat and she asked, 'Guess what animal he reminds me of?'

'A huge rat?'

'No, a wounded tiger that's limped off into the bush.'

'You're not feeling sorry for him, are you?' I asked, indignantly.

'Oh no,' cried Alice at once. I went on looking at her. 'Well, even you must feel a tiny bit sorry for him,' she said.

'I certainly don't,' I snapped. 'And just remember, a tiger's still a killer. When it gets better it will go back to its violent ways again.'

'I know that.'

'Actually I don't have one single atom of sympathy for him,' I said.

And I really didn't.

Instead, every time I saw Jake I'd feel my stomach getting all knotted up. I'd remember the way he'd ripped me apart behind my back. All those nasty spiteful games he'd played on me, and the way he'd set out to make my life so miserable that I'd want to leave this school. And worst of all — yes, definitely worst of all — was the way he'd acted as if he really enjoyed pulling my life to pieces.

No wonder the anger and fury I felt against him still blazed so strongly. I think it must have got right inside my bones. I was sure it would stay with me for good.

Feel sorry for Jake — never! In fact, for the first time in my life I wanted to see someone suffer. You might say a certain nastiness had crept into me. Well, if it had, that wasn't my fault. It was Jake who had put the nastiness there, wasn't it?

And he still made me uneasy. I feared that one

day his fortunes would revive again and he'd be back just when I was least expecting it. That's why I kept hoping that he'd leave my school. Surely even he couldn't go on day after day as an outcast. Especially after he'd been such a superstar before.

But then Alice, of all people, had to ruin everything.

CHAPTER TWENTY-FIVE

'I don't believe it.' I stared at her in horror, then I put my head in my hands for a moment. I felt suddenly very tired.

Alice and I were sitting in my bedroom. In the end she'd only been grounded for just over a week. But her mum had insisted on seeing the Headteacher and while she was there, Alice's mum had found out something ... which Alice then told me.

The person who'd grassed Alice up hadn't been Jake at all – no, it had been Leachy, our unbeloved caretaker. He'd passed by when we were talking about the smashed window – and heard Alice going on about how her mum would kill her. But he waited until his best pal, the Headteacher, had got back from his conference late that afternoon and then told him everything.

Of course, that was the very last thing I wanted to hear. Jake had to be guilty!

'Maybe Jake dropped you in it as well,' I suggested.

'I don't think so,' said Alice sadly.

'But he did sneak back to school and go and see Web-Head. I mean, it all fits.'

'I know,' said Alice, quietly. 'But he didn't do it.'

We were silent then for a bit. I was too shocked and depressed to utter a single word.

Finally Alice asked, 'So what are we going to do?'

'Do?'

'Yes.'

'Are we going to help Jake, do you mean? This person who tried to ruin my life.' I stopped. 'I think he deserves everything that's happened to him.'

There was silence again for a moment. Alice seemed lost in thought. I piped up again, 'And Alice, if we tell the class I was wrong in my accusation, well, I'll look a bit stupid.'

'No.'

'Yes I will. But more importantly, Jake could stage a comeback.'

'Oh, I don't think so.'

'You can't be sure though, can you? We'll always be looking over our shoulders, wondering if Jake's going to bounce back again. It'll be awful.'

'So you don't think we should do anything?'

'No, I don't,' I whispered.

I felt a little bit ashamed of what I was suggesting. But not much. I hated Jake so much more.

Alice got up and walked around my bedroom. She picked up my Avenger mask, looked at it for a few seconds. 'I just feel as if we're stitching Jake up,' she said, still holding the mask. 'What about if Jake's really sorry for what he's done to you?'

'He isn't.'

'How do you know?' She sat down beside me, the Avenger mask beside her. 'Look, Gareth, if Jake isn't sorry then I agree with you, we won't do anything to help him. Why should we? But I think it'd be well . . . dishonourable not to try first.'

'Dishonourable.' I smiled, picking up my Avenger mask. 'What are you going on about?'

But shortly afterwards I did agree to talk to Jake.

Big mistake.

CHAPTER TWENTY-SIX

Next lunch-time, Jake was sitting all by himself at the top of the back field as usual. Alice and I went up to him. He couldn't prevent a brief look of surprise from crossing his face. Up close I could see how blotchy his skin had become. His eyes looked all bloodshot too. For just a fraction of a second I did have a tiny flare of sympathy for him, but that was immediately extinguished by his greeting to us.

'So what do you two losers want then?'

I frowned heavily.

But Alice said, 'Jake, you've done some nasty things to people, especially Gareth. I – we – just wondered if you were sorry for what you did now?'

He put back his head and laughed. Loud, mocking laughter. Several people stared over at us. 'Do you want me to apologize, is that it?' Jake practically shouted. 'To him, to Garth? Never.'

'Call me Garth again and I'll punch you,' I cried.

'You'll punch me,' mocked Jake. 'Now I'm really shaking in my boots.' We glowered at each other.

'Oh no, stop this,' cried Alice. 'There's no point in you both just fighting each other again, is there?' She sounded frustrated and tearful.

'If I fight him I'll win,' declared Jake.

'Not this time,' I snapped.

Alice tugged at me. 'Come on, let's go.'

'Yeah, run away.'

'Let's just go, Gareth,' persisted Alice. 'Please.'
Alice and I left.

'That's right, scuttle off,' Jake called after us.
'And don't bother me again.'

A small crowd stood watching Alice and me
retreat. I was shaking with fury. 'We've made a
right show of ourselves,' I hissed. 'This is what
happens when you try to help someone like that.'

'He's just putting on a front,' said Alice quietly.

I stared at her. 'So he's a nice, kind person
really, is he?'

'No, of course not.' Alice shook her head
vigorously. 'I don't like him any more than you,
and I wanted to teach him a lesson. But with no
one talking to him all day and him just sitting at
the top of the field by himself every single lunch-
time – well, what sort of life is that?'

'Better than the one I had. No one's spreading
rumours about him and throwing things up at his
window in the middle of the night and . . .'

'Yes, all right. Look, let's just forget it.'

'And did you hear the way he called me Garth?'
A surge of ice-cold rage shot through me.

'I know . . .' began Alice.

'No you don't,' I scowled at her.

'Oh Gareth, that's not fair.'

'Catch you later,' I muttered. I was so choked

up with anger I didn't want to speak to anyone. Not even Alice. And anyway, she didn't really know what I was feeling. No one did.

That anger stayed with me for the rest of the day. It was as if I'd swallowed a very sharp stone and now it just lay on my chest. Every time I breathed in I could feel it.

Later that day the anger travelled upwards, leaving this extremely nasty bitter taste in my mouth. Even after I'd eaten, it was still there.

And all because of Jake. I kept telling myself that Grandad, Alice and I had defused him. He couldn't trouble me any more. I'd won. But it just didn't feel as if I had. Jake was still bugging me.

I only had to see him walking across the playground to get a flashback to something he'd said or done. And this rage would flood over me. I wasn't able to stop it either. It seemed to have a life of its own. Even at home I'd remember how bad Jake had made me feel. I just couldn't shake off those memories. They gnawed away inside me all the time.

There was only one solution. I had to make sure I never saw Jake again.

Alice came round my house that night – we'd been distinctly tetchy with each other lately and were trying to make up. Then I announced, 'I want Jake gone from our school for good.'

She looked shocked. 'But you don't speak to him any more. No one does.'

'He's still around though, isn't he? I think we should make another plan. Get rid of him for good.'

Alice looked at me, then said, softly, 'Oh, Gareth, can't we just forget about him now . . . ?'

'No,' I said shortly. Then I added, 'I'll only be free of him when he's gone.'

'Are you sure?' she asked in a cold low voice.

'What's that supposed to mean?' I demanded.

'Oh, forget it.'

'Funny how you're always defending him.'

'No, I'm not. What are you implying?'

'You like him, don't you? Go on, admit it.'

'Honestly, Gareth, you twist everything these days . . . you're just impossible.' Then she jumped to her feet and without another word tore downstairs.

'Aren't you going to help me?' I yelled after her.

'No, I'm not,' she yelled back.

I was very disappointed in Alice. She didn't understand that I couldn't just forget Jake. How could I when my heart was bursting with anger all day long.

Grandad would understand. He did know what I'd been through. And he'd help me make a fresh plan.

I'd often sensed him close by but I hadn't actually spoken to him for a few nights. So that night I held the Avenger mask in my hand and concentrated hard.

'Grandad, please try and get through tonight. I need to see you urgently. Thanks a lot.'

As usual, I had to fall asleep before anything happened. Then I woke up quite suddenly, and there was Grandad standing by the end of my bed. Before I could say anything he'd vanished away again.

'Grandad,' I cried, 'come back, Grandad.'

Nothing happened.

I called his name again.

And then my bedroom door eased open very slowly. 'Grandad?' I said hopefully.

I squinted into the darkness and saw . . . my

mum. 'Hello, love,' she said, as if she often wandered in for a chat at around this time. She stood by the end of my bed, just as Grandad had a few moments earlier.

'Did you hear me?' I asked.

She nodded.

Embarrassed now, I muttered, 'Sorry for waking you up.'

'Oh, I'm a light sleeper. Always have been. Used to sleep-walk a lot when I was your age, too. Walked out of the front door once you know.'

'I didn't know that.'

'Oh yes. I remember suddenly waking up outside in the pitch dark. I was very frightened until I saw your grandad running towards me in his pyjamas.'

I smiled.

'I was never so relieved in my whole life, to see him,' she cried.

'Grandad to the rescue,' I said.

'I dreamt about him the other night, you know.'

'Did you?'

'Yes, there he was, just the same . . .' Her voice trailed away. 'When you've known someone as special as that . . . you don't ever want to let him go.' She reached across and squeezed my hand. 'Let's help each other, shall we?'

After Mum had gone I lay awake thinking about what she'd said. I knew she missed Grandad too, of course. But I didn't know she'd been dreaming about him as well.

I nearly told her that Grandad had returned and was helping me.

Maybe one day I would. But first I needed to get him back properly again.

The following night I closed my eyes and whispered, 'Grandad, try and get through properly tonight, if you can. Thanks a million.'

And later that night I saw him, in the Avenger mask as usual – sitting on his chair.

'At last!' I cried.

'This materializing lark doesn't get any easier, you know.' He shook his head. 'Been trying to get through for days.'

'Can't tell you how good it is to see you,' I said. 'I've really missed you.'

'Missed you too,' said Grandad. 'Not that I've been very far away.'

Outside I couldn't even hear the distant rumble of traffic. Everything was totally still. There was a very definite chill in my bedroom too. But what did that matter – when I felt so warm inside?

Grandad said, 'Now, I know what ails you.'

'And you'll help me get rid of Jake for good?'

'Of course I'll help you,' said Grandad. 'Only . . . just hear me out first, will you?'

'Yes, all right,' I replied.

Then Grandad went on to tell me to do something so incredible . . .

'You really want me to do that . . . ?' I burst out.

'That's right.'

'But I couldn't. There must be some other way.'

'I'm afraid there really isn't. It's the hardest thing you'll ever do and the bravest . . . but I think you can manage it.'

I stared at him, frowning.

'Will you at least try?'

'No, sorry, but I don't think I can,' I said.

'At least give it a try.'

I hesitated.

'For my sake.'

Hard to refuse after Grandad said that. And I couldn't. Yet I was full of misgivings. I was confused too. What Grandad wanted me to do seemed all wrong.

But the following evening, I put his plan into action.

CHAPTER TWENTY-SEVEN

It was a foul night. I walked quickly to my destination. I just wanted to get this over with.

The sky above me roared with thunder. That was a bad omen, wasn't it?

I stopped outside Jake's house. My stomach turned over. Could I really go through with this?

A wave of fear rushed through me. It was so strong it took my breath away. I felt all shaky and unsteady.

No, I wasn't going any further. Instead I was going to return home. Maybe I'd try again tomorrow. Rain started splattering down. Yeah, I'd try another time when the weather was better.

Suddenly I didn't have one scrap of energy.

I very nearly turned back. Just three words stopped me.

I stood listening to the rain and the wind whispering in the trees – and those words which just flowed into my head: *'I am Avenger.'* And then I could see myself in my Avenger mask so clearly. It was as if over the past few days that picture had been growing inside my head. And now Avenger and I were smudging into each other. I wasn't just pretending any more . . . Avenger was actually part of me.

At that moment I could have done anything, even . . .

I rang on the doorbell of Jake's house. Muffled sounds of footsteps, a shadow looming up behind the glass and there he was – the person who'd tried to destroy me!

Jake looked really astonished to see me. 'What

do you want?' he asked, sounding both rude and suspicious. Before I could reply he said, with a sneering laugh, 'Come round to see if I'm sorry yet, have you?'

I gripped my hands into fists. This was going to be really really hard, but I could do this. I managed to keep my voice steady, 'Can I come in for a minute?'

'No, you can't,' he snapped. I feared he was going to bang the door in my face but instead he said abruptly, 'We'll talk in my bunker – but not for long. I've got better things to do than talk to you.'

'All right,' I agreed.

He opened the gate to his back garden, then strode across the grass. It had been raining so hard lately the grass was now not just heavy, but slimy mud. I half-ran, half-stumbled after him, my shoes sinking into the mud.

When he got to his bunker Jake opened the door. 'After you,' he said, politely. That should have made me suspicious.

But I was so intent on what I had to do, I wasn't at my most quick-witted, so I said, 'Thanks.' Before I knew what was happening the door had banged shut and the lock was slammed firmly into place.

I struggled to my feet. Through the window I saw Jake laughing at me.

'Let me out now!' I yelled at him.

'No way!' he shouted back, his face all screwed up with hatred.

I started kicking at the door. 'Shout all you like,' he cried. 'My parents have gone out and no one else will hear you.'

'You can't do this,' I cried.

'I just have,' said Jake, letting out a strangled laugh, then turning back and yelling at the top of his voice, 'You knew I didn't squeal on Alice. But you still let me take the blame. Well, now you can have a good, long think about that . . . Oh, and sleep well, won't you.'

'Jake, come back here,' I shouted. 'Jake!'

There was no answer.

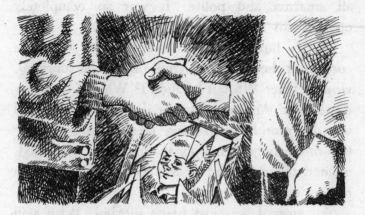

CHAPTER TWENTY-EIGHT

Jake couldn't mean to leave me here all night. Not even he was that twisted.

Was he?

I paced furiously around the shed. I kicked at the door as hard as I could. I opened my mouth and yelled at the top of my lungs. Someone just had to hear me. I listened until my ears burst. But it seemed nobody did.

I was burning up with frustration now. I was trapped here, and all because of Grandad. It really wasn't one of his better ideas. No – I couldn't blame Grandad. It was me. I should have realized Jake was up to something when he started acting all smarmy and polite. It was so completely obvious now.

Exactly how long was Jake going to keep me cooped up here? He'd let me out in the morning, wouldn't he? What if he didn't? What if he never came back? And no one ever discovered me, until one day months from now, Jake's mum, noticing the most awful stink emanating from the shed, opened the door and in the corner, discovered a rotting corpse, me?

No, stop. I was just being morbid. What will actually happen is: later on tonight, Mum will wonder where I am and ring up some of my friends. She might even phone Jake.

No, she knows Jake and I aren't mates any more. So she probably won't contact him. But she'll call the police, all right, and they might do a door-to-door search. Would they think of looking here?

I began pacing about again. Then I spotted that large picture of Jake on the wall – the one I'd noticed the first time I'd come here and which Jake had wanted me to keep quiet about. Suddenly I grabbed the picture and hurled it into the bin. Best place for it.

I could hear the rain drumming against the window. It sounded extremely loud. I was getting cold too. Was Jake in bed now? I bet he was safely tucked up, while I'm here . . .

A roll of thunder shook the walls of the shed. I just couldn't stay here all night. There must be a way out. I examined the door again. It really wasn't that strong. I got ready to run against it with all my might. 'Here goes,' I whispered to myself. And then . . . the door gave a small click and sprang open, apparently all by itself.

I belted outside. Jake was already disappearing down the garden. 'Thanks for nothing,' my voice rang out through the rain.

Jake turned round and yelled back, 'Got some good news for you. I'm leaving your school, going to the other one in the town.'

That was exactly what I had wanted: Jake out of my school for good.

'Thought that would please you,' he cried. Oddly enough, it didn't. Instead all I could hear was Grandad's voice urging me to tell Jake why I'd come here.

I didn't know if I could now – or even if I wanted to.

Jake started moving away again. I cried out, suddenly, 'Don't you want to know why I came round here again tonight?'

'Not really.' But he stopped.

For a moment we both stood there in silence, the rain streaming down our faces. 'What I wanted to say to you was . . .' I took a massive intake of breath. 'That I'm sorry for not telling everyone you didn't squeal on Alice. I should have done that. And I'll tell everyone tomorrow morning.' I was talking too fast. But Jake heard what I'd said all right.

'Taken you long enough,' he cried. 'You should have told everyone weeks ago. You stitched me up over that.'

I wanted to retaliate that what I'd done was nothing, absolutely nothing, compared to all the things he'd done to me. Why should I eat any more humble pie for him? But I restrained myself, and in the end just said, 'I'll tell everyone tomorrow, that's a promise.'

'It doesn't matter anyhow as I'm not going back. My mum's already been to that school . . .'

'There's something else,' I said. Here it was now. The thing I really didn't want to say. It was definitely the hardest thing I'd ever had to utter. But Grandad had insisted. 'I . . . I . . .' Then, all in a rush again. 'I want you to know, Jake, I didn't like the things you did. And what you said. They made me feel really bad, actually. But I don't hold a grudge against you. I did before, but I don't now.' After saying this, I squelched over the mud-soaked lawn and stretched out my hand to him.

Jake just stood there, rain dripping from his brow, looking as if he couldn't believe what was happening. I suppose it was pretty incredible. But he didn't shake my hand.

A bolt of lightning suddenly erupted across the steely grey sky. In that flash I could see that Jake was standing there, all stooped over and shaking slightly like a very old man.

Then, over a great crack of thunder he shrieked, 'Just go away and leave me alone,' and pelted into his bunker, slamming the door shut behind him.

So that was that. That last speech had been the hardest thing I'd ever had to say. But it hadn't worked. There was nothing else to do now.

I stood there in the cold rain, knowing I should go home but not wanting to for some strange reason. Then I heard this high-pitched yell from the bunker. It sounded as if Jake had just hurt himself. I tore up the garden and sneaked a look through the window. Jake was sitting on the floor, his head in his hands. He suddenly gazed up and saw me staring in at him. He scrambled unsteadily to his feet.

I opened the door. 'Just heard you . . . are you all right?'

'Yeah, I'm fine.' But even as he said this, tears were spurting all down his face. He hastily brushed them aside, then got out his hankie and blew his nose like a trumpet.

I hovered awkwardly, noticing suddenly he'd taken the photo of himself out of the bin. It was under his arm now.

'Sorry about bunging your picture in the bin . . . I got a bit cooped up in there.'

Jake jammed the hankie back into his pocket and declared, 'You thought it was big-headed of me, putting a picture of myself up, didn't you?' he demanded accusingly.

'Er, yeah, all right, I did.'

He gave me a strange, little smile. 'Actually, that picture is here to remind me who I am.'

'Say that again,' I said.

He edged a couple of steps nearer to me. 'At my old school – yes, in Felixstowe' – he gave a small bow – 'you'll be amazed to learn I wasn't actually very popular. No good at sports and no good at schoolwork either. By the way, when you saw me slipping off to see Mrs Webber that day, I was arranging to have extra lessons because of my extreme thickness.'

'Oh, right,' I said quietly.

'But I wanted to be in with everyone. I was a

bit like Tim, I suppose. Only I was really desperate. People can smell that. It turns them right against you as well. You just become a big joke. And people were always laughing at me . . .' His voice rose. 'They never gave me a chance. I had a bad image and that was it.

'I was stuck, until we moved here. It was like crossing into another world. I could start all over again, wipe out who I was and give myself a totally different character.'

Jake said this in such a matter-of-fact voice. As if extinguishing your old self and being someone quite different was an everyday occurrence.

He went on. 'I spent weeks planning out who I was going to be. Someone cool and very sure of himself. I based my character a bit on a boy at my old school who everyone respected. But he had lived in Felixstowe all his life. I decided to give myself a life on the back streets of London – I figured most of you would never even have been to London so I was safe there. And I practised my cockney accent every night . . . I was proud of that.'

I nodded. 'Yeah, it was really natural.'

'I also had this picture taken of me looking cool, so I wouldn't forget who I was now. Each night I'd look at it and remember. Then I walked into your school for the first time. I was so nervous, I can't tell you, but it worked, didn't it?' He was looking right at me now.

'Yes it did,' I agreed. 'From the start you were a top man. By the way, when you were talking into your mobile phones, who were you . . . ?'

'No one,' interrupted Jake. 'There was never anyone there. Well, in my head there was – but nowhere else.'

'Amazing,' I said. 'Well, you had us all fooled for a bit.'

'Oh, it went even better than I'd dreamed,' he admitted. 'Best of all, though, I had a mate. Someone I thought I could really trust – until he crucified me . . .' He stopped, accusingly.

Even after all this time I could feel his bitterness. 'I'm sorry . . .' I began.

But he interrupted. 'I went sick inside when I saw what you were doing. And after that, whenever I saw you I'd see them too. All those other people who'd made fun of me. In my eyes, you were just as bad as they were. No, worse, because I'd trusted you and you betrayed me.'

He stopped, as if expecting me to cut in here but I didn't. I just shrugged my shoulders in a defeated sort of way.

He turned from me and started staring at the floor. 'Doesn't excuse what I did to you, though. I knew it was really bad and nasty. But I wasn't just getting my revenge on you . . . it was all those other ones. And once the spite gets into your blood . . . well, the nastiness becomes like a habit. You just can't shake it off.'

'Yes,' I said slowly. 'I can see how that might happen.'

And I could.

Then, with a deep sigh, he sank down on the floor. 'I'm not sorry it's over, you know,' he said in a low mutter and without raising his eyes. 'Nothing wears you out like pretending. And all the time I was watching my parents, afraid they'd let slip something and blow it all sky high. Sorry for what I did to you, though, Gareth.'

It was quite a shock hearing him call me by my real name again. Once more I stretched out my hand to him. Only he didn't realize at first, as he wasn't looking at me. I don't think he could. When he did he let out a cry of amazement. 'You really want to shake my hand?'

'Yeah.'

'You're mad.'

'I know.'

'Oh, why not?' he cried, getting back on his feet. He walked heavily over to me. We shook hands. Then he choked back a sob and turned away. 'I'd like to be on my own now,' he muttered.

'Yeah, sure,' I said. 'See you tomorrow then.'

'Maybe,' he whispered.

As soon as I got back home I rang Alice and started to tell her what had happened.

'You went to see Jake?' She sounded shocked and fearful. 'You two didn't have another fight, did you?'

I related what had actually happened. She then became so silent I had to ask if she was still there.

'I'm here all right,' she cried.

'You're very shocked, aren't you?'

'I am . . . and I'm not.'

'Explain please.'

'Well, I didn't think you'd go round to see Jake tonight. But I thought you would, one day.'

'Did you really?'

'Oh yes, because the way you've been acting lately, being all spiteful and hard about Jake — well, it wasn't like you.'

Actually, it was a bit like me. Whether I always had some nastiness lurking inside me, or lately I'd just invited it in, I wasn't sure. But knowing how I had this horrible side to me actually made it easier to start forgiving Jake.

'I thought I might call for Jake tomorrow,' I said.

'Oh Gareth, that's a really nice gesture.'

'Oh, shut up.'

We both laughed. But just before Alice rang off she said, 'I'm sorry, but I've just got to say this: I really admire you for what you did tonight.'

I couldn't help revelling a bit in Alice's praise. But I knew the person Alice really should have been admiring was my grandad. He was the one who'd put the idea into my head. He'd said, 'You've got to stop carrying this anger around inside you, as it's not good for you at all. You'll have to let it go.'

'Just how do I do that?' I had demanded.

Quick as a flash Grandad had replied, 'The best way possible. Give the anger right back to Jake. Tell him you don't bear a grudge any more. The slate is wiped clean . . .'

'What!' I'd exclaimed. 'I could never, ever do that.'

'Why not?'

'Because he's not at all sorry . . . he doesn't deserve to be forgiven.'

'But remember, and this is very important,' Grandad had said, 'you're doing this for your sake – not his.'

I hadn't seen what Grandad meant then. But now I could. It was as if something which had been dragging me down for weeks had just vanished away. I felt – and this probably sounds totally daft – much lighter.

Anyway, that's how I felt. And I couldn't wait to tell Grandad what had happened today. I'd only been asleep for a couple of minutes, or so it seemed, when I saw him sitting in his chair. Only this time he wasn't dressed as Avenger.

No, he was back to being Grandad as I'd known him. I just thought he fancied a change and didn't think any more about it. I burbled away about the evening's events.

When I'd finished he said, 'That's smashing, absolutely smashing. What you did tonight . . . well, don't let anyone tell you forgiveness is weakness. Forgiving someone demands so much strength . . . And I know. Those people who'd sneered and mocked me when I wanted to be a wrestler . . . I just couldn't forgive them. They tried to make friends but I was too eaten up with anger until . . .'

'Until you discovered the magic of saying, "I am Avenger",' I interrupted.

Grandad smiled. 'That's right. The pain inside me had got so bad I thought, I've got to do something. So that's when, for the very first time, I imagined I was still wearing my Avenger mask.'

'And you said those three magic words.'

'Over and over. And then I had all the power I needed to make peace with my foes. I was in a total daze afterwards, of course. Had I really done that?'

'That's exactly how I feel,' I cried excitedly. 'I've done things as Avenger I never imagined possible for me.'

'There's so much more inside us than we realize,' Grandad said. 'But sometimes it's only when we put on a mask that we can see that.'

'Well, thanks for telling me about Avenger,' I said quietly. 'Don't know what I'd have done if you hadn't come back.'

He leaned forward. 'Will you help me now, Gareth?'

CHAPTER TWENTY-NINE

'Of course I will. Anything you want,' I cried. But I was puzzled. How on earth could I help Grandad?

'Going to shock you now,' he said, smiling at me. 'Remember that night when you called me back?'

'How could I forget it?'

'Well, actually you didn't.'

'What!'

'No, I let you think that, but here's the truth now. When I found out that I'd, as they say, passed away, I was hopping mad. I didn't want to leave your mum and Lisa and you.' He sighed heavily, and more to himself than me, murmured, 'What a thief time is.' Then he went on, 'So I decided I wasn't budging and stayed right here.'

'And you never left the house at all,' I whispered.

'No.'

'But that's brilliant. Hey, Grandad — you rebel.' He laughed.

'And all those times I sensed you nearby . . .'

'Oh, I was there all right, trying to learn how to materialize.'

'You do it very well now,' I said.

'Yes, I think I've finally got the hang of it,' he said, proudly.

'And you'll stay for good now, won't you?' I asked eagerly.

'Actually I am ready to go now,' said Grandad, his voice hardly even a whisper.

I stared at him so shocked I was speechless at first. Then I leaned forward. 'Listen, Grandad, I'll go to bed earlier – straight after tea, in fact. Then at night I won't be so sleepy and we can spend hours and hours chatting away. You can tell me some more of your brilliant stories. It'll be just superb. You know it will. So come on, stay with me.'

He shook his head. 'Can't.'

'Why not?'

'Why!' exclaimed Grandad, his voice shaking. 'Because there's a whole new world out there waiting for you . . . and you won't see any of it stuck in here with me, will you?'

I felt a lump rising in my throat. 'I don't care about any of that. I'll never find anyone like you.'

'Yes you will,' replied Grandad. 'I think you already have.' He gave a little chuckle.

'But I just want us back like before.'

'And so do I, lad . . . but I'm afraid that can't happen.'

Tears started to well up in my eyes.

'Come on now,' said Grandad. 'Think of all those extra weeks we've had together – against all the rules, you know. That didn't stop us though, did it? But now . . .' His voice started to shake again. 'You've got so much to look forward to, and I don't want you to miss a moment of it.'

Then he got out of his chair and half-walked, half-floated over to the window. He stared out into the still night, then said, 'I am Avenger.' He looked across at me. 'Will you help me, Gareth – and say it too. It'll give me some extra courage which I could do with at the moment.'

I turned away from him. 'You go if you like, but I'm not helping. I don't want to lose you.'

'Gareth.' Grandad spoke my name very gently.

I looked up.

He didn't say anything at first, just smiled deep into my eyes. Then he said, slowly, 'We shan't ever lose each other . . . not you and me. Now, please help me.'

I swallowed hard, then whispered, very faintly, 'I am Avenger.'

'Oh, say it so that I can hear it,' said Grandad in such a cranky voice I had to smile. 'Come on now, say it properly for me.'

'I am Avenger,' I cried out.

'That's more like it,' said Grandad. 'Now say it for me again.'

'I am Avenger,' I cried. And all at once, Grandad started growing much fainter.

'Grandad,' I called, 'I just wanted you to know I do feel stronger now . . . and all because of you.' I don't know for certain if he heard me. I think he did. But the next thing I knew he'd melted completely away into the darkness.

For a few seconds his sweet-smelling soap lingered in the air. Then that faded away too and my bedroom seemed suddenly full of emptiness. It still does sometimes.

But I've got good friends now, like Tim. He comes round (or I visit him) most weekends. As for Jake . . . Well, the very next day I told everyone that Jake hadn't grassed on Alice.

Afterwards Jake said to me, 'I never thought you'd actually do that.' Then we shook hands again. Since then we've become mates. Not exactly as we were before, but we're getting along all right and I never thought I'd be writing that about Jake.

As for Alice . . . Well, she's become dead special to me, actually. And if I write any more I'll start blushing really badly, so I won't.

And what about Grandad? Have I ever . . . ? No, I've never seen him again. But you know what: Grandad was right. I haven't lost him.

I'll never lose him.

He'll live on inside my heart, for ever.

SOME THINGS YOU MAY NOT KNOW ABOUT
PETE JOHNSON:

- He used to be a film critic on Radio One. Sometimes he saw three films a day.

- He has met a number of famous actors and directors, and collects signed film pictures.

- Pete's favourite book when he was younger was *One Hundred and One Dalmations*. Pete wrote to the author of this book, Dodie Smith. She was the first person to encourage Pete to be a writer. *Traitor* is dedicated to her.

- Once when Pete went to a television studio to talk about his books he was mistaken for an actor and taken to the audition room. TV presenter Sarah Greene also once mistook Pete for her brother.

- When he was younger Pete used to sleepwalk regularly. One night he woke up to find himself walking along a busy road in his pyjamas.

- Pete's favourite food is chocolate. He especially loves Easter eggs and received over forty this year.

- Pete's favourites of his own books are *The Ghost Dog* and *How to Train Your Parents*. The books he enjoys reading most are thrillers and comedies.

- Pete likes to start writing by eight o'clock in the morning. He reads all the dialogue aloud to see if it sounds natural. When he's stuck for an idea he goes for a long walk.

- He carries a notebook wherever he goes. 'The best ideas come when you're least expecting them' he says.

TRAITOR
Pete Johnson

Have the bullies pushed someone too far?

What would *you* do if a gang of bullies
decided to waylay you on your way home
from school, demanding money?
Would you pay up?

That's what Tom, Mia and Oliver
do – at first. Ashamed of being victims,
united in their fear of the gang, they feel
powerless to do anything else. But as the
pressure builds more and more, a terrible
suspicion begins to surface: could one of
the three friends be *helping* the bullies?
And if so, just who is… the traitor?

A perceptive and highly credible tale of
bullying and friendship from award-winning
Pete Johnson, author of *The Ghost Dog*,
Rescuing Dad and many other titles.

ISBN 0 440 86438 0